MW00937435

To Haly

Best Wishes

8/15/294

AIKIDO
AU REVOIR

Published by Basswood Press

Library of Congress Control Number Pending

ISBN – 10:1492377465
ISBN – 13:978-1492377467

© 2013 Basswood Press
Manufactured in the United States of America

AIKIDO AU REVOIR

By

Daniel Linden

Also Available by DANIEL LINDEN

Non-fiction

On Mastering Aikido – 2nd Edition
9 Dialogs on Principles
(2004, 2010)
Journey – On Mastering Ukemi
(2010)

Fiction

The Content of Character (2011)

The Aikido Mysteries

*The Aikido Caper 1 (*2011)
The Aikido-Ka 2 (2012)
Aikido Anejo 3 (2012)
The Aikido Sensei 4 (2013)
The Aikido Mysteries – The First Three Novels
(2013)

AIKIDO AU REVOIR

An Aikido Mystery

By

Daniel Linden

For Laurie, with love.
We'll always have Paris,
But we'll dream of Nice.

Chapter 1

"What's a good looking hunk of man like you doing in a place like this?"

I knew the voice. Bogart, of course, Bogart... But the words were being said with the husky, feminine allure of young Kathleen Turner. I froze.

"Monique?" I spun around and there she was, grinning from ear to ear. Her blond hair was in a different do, but her blue eyes were shining just like the last time I'd seen her... the time we'd said goodbye. She threw herself at me and I caught her on the rise and hugged her with a ferociousness that I'd forgotten. She hugged me back just as fiercely.

"Oh, Parker, damn, it's good to see you," and just like that she was kissing me full on the mouth and no holds barred.

We stood like that for eternity. Then slowly I settled her back to the sidewalk.

"C'mon," she said, grabbing my arm. "The gang's all here and they're going to want to say hello." She dragged me down the sidewalk and I saw Martin Scarlotti looking up at me across a table filled with the remains of a French lunch for the rich and famous. He stood as soon as he recognized me, but not as quickly as the movie star, Thad Deep. He was already pushing through the ropes and the crowd to get to the sidewalk and when I walked up he threw his arms around me like we were long lost brothers.

9

"Sensei! I just knew you'd make it!"

I doubted it. I hadn't heard from him in at least two years and the last time we'd been together he'd left without saying goodbye. He was just a big Hollywood star doing his bit.

Martin Scarlotti, my old boss, was standing and offering me his hand. I took it and we grinned at each other.

"I was hoping you'd call," I said. "I really enjoyed making *Above the Fray*. I would have been happy to work with you and Harvey again as Martial Arts Coordinator for the sequel, *Above the Fray 2 - Grab My Wrist*!" I shook my head and gave him a slight grin.

He leaned close so only I would hear. "There isn't any Aikido in this movie, Parker. Damn, there's hardly any martial arts at all. It's all car chases, guns, shoot outs, helicopter crashes, bus crashes, hot babes chasing around... I mean, there's hardly a discernible plot. But it's what the studio wanted. I would have called you if I'd needed you. Trust me."

I nodded.

We were in Cannes at the famous film festival and had just run into each other accidentally.

It's a long story.

Chapter 2

Several months back I'd been contacted about teaching a couple Aikido seminars at a dojo in the South of France on the Riviera. I know, don't even say it. It's tough, but somebody's got to do it.

It was actually the result of having had an extended affair with a beautiful French woman, a visiting Aikido student. It had been decades ago. She had continued to train when she'd finally returned to France and was now teaching Aikido herself in Villefranche Sur Mer, a picturesque old village situated between Nice and Monaco on the Riviera. Corrine is a natural teacher and gravitated to being a sensei as easily as she taught her elementary school classes for the French government school system. She is a fifth degree black belt, a godan, and has a wonderful dojo in the old tourist section of the small town.

She came back to the U.S. on a vacation last year. We'd connected again – she was never shy about looking for a free place to stay - and afterward she asked me to come teach the seminars. One of the advantages and disadvantages about living in Orlando is that everyone comes here eventually. If not for a vacation at Disney and Epcot, then they come for a business conference at the largest convention venue in the world. One thing we have plenty of is hotel rooms, for those who choose to stay in them.

Corrine Royer, I call her Kara, showed up on my door step in June. She'd looked just the same as the last time I'd seen her except her hair was gray. I mean it, she had not changed one little bit in twenty years except for the hair. If she had bothered to color it and wear it the same I would have believed I'd slipped into a time warp. But there is certainly precedence, after all. Bridgette Bardot was a stunning woman even into her fifties, and the French do have that expression, 'a woman of a certain age'…

I invited her in. She'd had her suitcase and asked if she could stay for a week. I asked her if she minded the dog. She said, no. I said, yes. We practiced Aikido every morning, she went to Disney, Epcot, Universal Studios, Sea World. etc. every day and we had a very nice week.

When she left she kissed me goodbye and I didn't expect to hear from her again for another decade, but she surprised me the following week with the invitation.

So now we were in France.

I looked over my shoulder and saw Curtis walking down the sidewalk with Patrice and Jacques, two of Kara's students. They were a little surprised to see me there with the Hollywood celebrities, but the French are nothing if not cool. Blasé would be more accurate. Thad Deep looked up surprised when he saw Curtis and this time he actually jumped over the rope and ran up to him causing a huge outcry from passers-by.

"Thad Deep! Thad Deep!" It was a cry akin to a battle charge and for a moment I thought Curtis would be doing Aikido for real out in the middle of the Cannes sidewalk, but then Thad hurried him to the security of the roped-off sidewalk café. I motioned to Patrice and Jacques to come over, but they waved and looked the absolute soul of boredom. People had surrounded the area to get a glimpse of the celebrities and security guards were busy asking people to move along, all done with typical French insouciance.

I looked over to see Curtis shaking Martin's hand. Harry gave him a huge hug and both Thad and Valenzuela were smiling brightly at him. I realized that they had not seen him ambulatory since he had fallen saving the first *Above the Fray* movie. His wounds had been awful and he had spent months recovering from the horrible cut made by the man who had tried to kill Thad Deep with a samurai sword. Monique leaned over and whispered in my ear.

"It's great to see him up and around. Is he completely recovered?"

"Yes. He's back to teaching and working for NASA. He seems to be doing very well, but he's having marital problems. It's why he came with me." I was being drawn in by her perfume, so subtle, just the merest hint...

"What are you doing here? You're not a film junkie. What are you doing in Cannes?"

"I'm teaching a seminar just down the coast, by Nice. It's in the next village past it, Villefranche Sur Mer. This weekend and next weekend, you know... How are you, Money?"

She leaned her head against my chest and looked up at me and smiled. "I'm better now. Can you come to the premier of *Above the Fray 2 – Grab My Wrist!*? It will be a lot of fun, it's the World Premier, you know. You could be my date!"

I smiled at her and said, "I don't have a tuxedo."

She punched my shoulder and laughed. "Right! You can rent a tux, Parker."

"When is it?"

"Tomorrow night."

I thought about it and realized it would be impossible if I was going to take the seminar seriously. People expect to have a social evening with a visiting Sensei and class would run until 9:00 PM, then we would be expected to attend a dinner.

"I'm sorry Money, I've got plans I can't break. I am working here, you know."

She smiled sadly then and I realized she had not been kidding or playing. She had really wanted me to be her date. I saw it in her eyes and in the small lines that formed on each side of her mouth. It surprised me.

"Hey, what's up?"

She shrugged and looked away, but then pointed her chin and tugged lightly on my arm. I followed and we walked into the foyer of the hotel. She had to stop and show some kind of I.D. to the hotel security person, but then we were inside in the quiet opulence of old French architecture. We walked over to a set of couches in front of a cold fireplace and sat. She'd not let go of me and we were still arm in arm.

Monique Keller is an old flame. We'd met on the set of the original remake of *Above the Fray* and had become quite close. I'd even asked her to marry me, but it had not worked out, and even though I believed that the flames had finally died, sitting here with her was causing a powerful rush of emotion to rise in me.

"Parker, do you really want to hear this? We haven't talked in a year." She looked deep in my eyes and saw that I did. "Well, you get tired, you know?" She leaned her head on my shoulder and we watched people walk by through the big glass windows that overlooked the Mediterranean Sea.

"I think I have been wondering if it's all worth it, lately… going to bed alone and getting up alone and never really arriving… Do you know what I mean?"

"I do," I said. "But in a lot of ways you have arrived. You are the Assistant Producer of a huge motion picture with an amazing director and real stars... And you have a very impressive resume now. If it matters at all, I really liked your Civil War film... If that isn't arriving I don't know what is. Unless you aren't talking about your career success..."

"Maybe I am, well, maybe I'm not. I'm lonely, Parker. Even with all these people around me constantly I'm lonely. I think about you all the time."

I must have looked my surprise.

"I mean it. God if you knew all the times I've wanted to call you... and the creeps out there, and even the nice guys... but there aren't any like you. You know that, don't you, Big Fella? Well, there are occasional... flings, but you are the only man I have really connected with. I think I made a mistake." She looked searchingly in my eyes.

This was all coming way too fast. I watched people walk past on the boulevard and thought about how tired I was from the long flight and the jet lag. I thought about teaching the seminar. But I also remembered how being with her made me feel and what her love was like. It was like Christmas; every day full of surprises and warmth, laughter and love.

I had taught the morning class and Corrine told me that in France during seminars they traditionally break for three hours over lunch. I'd grabbed a sandwich at a bakery on the street and Patrice and Jacques had piled Curtis and me into Jacques' car for a tour of the Riviera. I'm not certain if they had even known that the famous film festival was taking place, we had simply driven down the highway past Nice and Antibes and into Cannes. Jacques had decided to stop and suggested we take a walk along the sea, but before we had even gone down to the beach we had been grabbed by the Hollywood celebrities.

I looked up to see him looking through the window at me. He pointed to his wristwatch and made a motion of two fingers walking. I nodded and pointed to the doors.

"Monique, I have to go. I really do, but I want to talk to you again and very soon. Do you have a number where I can reach you?"

"Oh, yes. Wait…"

I got out my phone and told her my number. She called me and as soon as my phone began to ring I thumbed it off and entered her name. She did the same.

"Parker… I'm sorry. I didn't mean to come off as…"

I leaned over and kissed her on the mouth. I held her and in a moment she relaxed and responded. Then she hugged me and we both knew it was alright.

"I will call you as soon as I get a handle on what's expected of me and what free time I can arrange."

"I know," she said. "I know you will."

Still, as I walked to the massive doors I remembered I had not changed my phone number in ten years. She could have called me any time.

Chapter 3

Jacques drove us back over the hills to the small town on the bay. Afternoon sun glinted off the shimmering Mediterranean Sea and caused the colors to drift between sapphire blue to blue gray and even odd shades of jade green as the clouds danced and brought shadows across the water. We passed the harbor in Nice and then slowly crawled up and around the peninsula separating Nice from Villefranche Sur Mer.

The dojo is in a small street, what most Americans would call an alley, but I don't think it would have translated the same here. It is just a small, pretty, block-long street. Lofts were wedged in between some local businesses and upstairs apartments that overlook the street with balconies and clothes hanging on lines to dry. Her number is 23 Rue de Laurie and the tiny street is two blocks east of the Rue de May off Rue Volti.

We had to park up on the main road, the Rue de la Victoire, just where it turns off the lower corniche, the coastal highway in English. This road has as many different names as there are cities and towns. Here it is Av. Albert 1, but in Nice it is far more fancifully named the Blvd Princesse Grace de Monaco. I can tell you this because they all made me memorize it, not once, but several times. I guess the idea of a big American wandering around lost without a clue as to where he is supposed to be made them all nervous.

Each time we parked they made sure I knew all the landmarks and street names, and even wrote them down for me.

In retrospect it is probable that Kara told her students that I have a tendency to wander and have no regards for where I go or when I need to return. We had traveled to Istanbul together many years before and while she explored the Topkapi Palace I had found a taxi driver who spoke English and had asked him to take me everywhere in the old city he had never before taken a tourist. It took Kara hours of frantic searching before she considered the idea that I was probably back in the hotel at the bar, which is where she finally tracked me down. After that she figured out it's a good idea to keep track of me when I'm off the clock and wandering.

We walked slowly down Rue Volti while I window grazed in every bakery and patisserie on the street. I couldn't possible eat every wonderful thing I saw, but I could dream. We ran into Philippe Tessier, another of Kara's students. He was hurrying toward the dojo and he joined us. He is Professor of Paleontology at the University of Nice Sophia Antipolis. We continued toward the dojo and Patrice and Jacques spoke slowly in English explaining that there are several rare anthropological digs right in Nice. It was beginning to rain and I was more interested in the pastries and the breads and cakes in the many bakeries we passed than in bones thousands of years old. We began to hurry and when we turned onto Rue de May and then made the slight jog onto Rue de Laurie we found a number of students standing outside the dojo doors and deep in conversation.

I stepped up and saw immediately that there had been a break-in. The conversation slowly stopped as I stepped up to the door and knelt down and examined the lock. Wood lay on the ground and there were pieces of the latch plate lying on the ground. I'd worked with my Grandpa Spenser in his lock shop for enough summers to know that a broken latch plate is very unusual. Latch plates are usually the second strongest part of a lock. They keep the bolt secure. It appeared that someone had used something very hard and strong to pry open the doors, shattering the heavy oak frame and breaking both the lock and the plate.

I looked inside. Nothing seemed to be upset, but I called Philippe and Jacques to me.

"Can you tell if anything is missing?"

"There is nothing to steal," Jacques told me. "Nothing. We keep nothing there. All money is paid by, um, you know the bank draft? The wire draft?"

"Direct deposit," I said.

"Yes. And we sell nothing... no gi, no hakama, nothing..."

"Can you take your shoes off, and look around inside to see if anything is out of place before the police arrive?"

"Bof," Philippe snorted. "Police will not come for such as this." He looked around at the other students who had moved up and out of the rain, but apparently none of them spoke English because he needed to translate what he'd said. Once he had they all nodded in agreement.

"We will need to go to the Gendarmerie and then wait while we make out the report and then wait while it is questioned, and then wait while it is processed, and then wait to speak to someone who will be bored and not care and then we will be sent away. Why bother?"

"Insurance?" I asked.

"It is only a lock. Philippe shrugged as only the French can and then explained what he'd said to the others.

Several nodded and several spoke and then Jacques came back and he too shrugged.

"Nothing is wrong."

At that everyone proceeded in, took their shoes off and headed to the changing rooms. Class was due to begin in twenty minutes.

I knelt down again and looked at the pieces of the latch. I opened my Leatherman tool – I never travel without it, not anywhere – and removed the lock from the door. It was heavy and old and the door was strong. In my hand the thing felt like it weighed five pounds. I tried to figure out if it could be repaired and after a few minutes of manipulating the spring latch and the deadbolt I figured it was still in good shape. They would need a new latch plate, though.

I signaled for Philippe to come over to me and asked him if there were a locksmith anywhere around and explained what we needed. He went off to talk to a young man who left the mat and came back a few minutes later in street clothes. He took the pieces of the latch plate and left. I went to change my clothes and when I came out of the changing room I saw Kara standing in the middle of the viewing area and she was very angry. Apparently there was something missing after all.

Someone clapped their hands and then all the students rushed to sit on their knees in seiza. The room fell absolutely silent. Kara turned and walked to her office and I did the only thing I was supposed to do.

I waited. I gave the students a moment to collect themselves, then stepped out to the mat area. There were far more people here than there had been for the morning class. I estimated well over a hundred. The students were lined up in rows ready to bow in and there were three full rows that extended the length of the mat area.

Frankly, I was shocked. I was also pleased. I walked out and discovered to my dismay that something was, indeed, missing. The kakemono – the scroll that says Aikido in Japanese – was gone. It had been there when we'd left the dojo for lunch and now it was missing. I bowed anyway and the students coordinated their bow with mine and we began class.

While they were working out in pairs I wandered back to the tokanoma - the shrine - and looked to see if it had fallen or been placed on the mat, but the kakemono was missing. Kara was looking at me when I turned around, so I walked over to the edge of the mat to speak with her.

""Did someone steal this?" I asked.

"What else could it be?" she said. "There is nothing else missing."

"But why? Was it something special?"

"No. At least I don't think anyone would find it so valuable…" It was done by Tamura Sensei just before he died. But it was small, nothing fancy and it was mine… Who would do this?"

I didn't know what to say and had other more pressing responsibilities, so I turned and walked around the mat offering suggestions and compliments as I went. I used the word bon – good, I used a slight shrug and one hand shaking, I nodded a bit and then stopped surprised and blurted, "That's very nice!"

The big man smiled and said, "Thank you, Sensei." His voice had a nice lilt and his grin was genuine. "Seamus Murphy," he said and offered me his hand.

"Nice to see you here," I said. "You're a long way from Ireland."

"I'm from Texas, actually, Ah, and the pleasure would be all mine."

I laughed and we spoke for a moment and then I slapped him lightly on the shoulder and moved on. I watched

Philippe working with a young woman in white gi and no hakama. She seemed very inexperienced, but she was very pretty and I was certain she would have plenty of help from more experienced partners. I continued to circulate and evaluate. It was a typical group and I watched some good technique, some mediocre, and some seriously misplaced ego. It was just like any place you go, I surmised, and then went back to the front of the class and clapped my hands. We had a long class ahead and I began to teach my own personal approach to the practice of Aikido.

Chapter 4

"You said that Tamura Sensei made the kakemono and gave it to you?"

"No, not exactly. I had the scroll already. The split bamboo roll, you know? I bought it at a house sale and asked Tamura Sensei to do a kanji for our little dojo. Philippe had some good rice paper and so Sensei took a brush and some ink and did the kanji. I put it on the roll of split bamboo and that was all it was, just some old bamboo and three symbols on rice paper." She was still angry, but now the loss was beginning to make her a little weepy as well. We were in a nice restaurant in Vieux Nice. Most of Kara's black belts had elected to accompany us to the place and were scattered around eating at small tables in a reserved area. All were close enough that with effort we could communicate, but equally distant enough so we could speak privately. I was sharing a bottle of rosé, the region's specialty, with Kara and it was having only a slight effect.

I thought about the single kanji that was framed and sitting on the tokanoma at the head of my dojo back in Orlando. My old sensei, Hunter James, had given it to me when he had closed his dojo and quit teaching. It was only one kanji, the symbol ki, but it had been given to him by O'Sensei himself. I treasured the small bit of ink and rice paper and wondered briefly if I was being foolish just leaving it sit there in my unlocked dojo.

"Kara, I saw it when I bowed the class in and out this morning, but honestly didn't pay it much attention. Was there anything special about it? Think. Was there anything at all that would make it valuable?"

"No," she said. "Not really. It was thirty centimeters wide, and maybe fifty long. You know, tall? And the kanji was on paper twenty centimeters by thirty-five. In America you say eight by fourteen inches. The bamboo was very old, I think, and finely split so it rolled up smooth, but once Tamura Sensei did the Aikido kanji and I glued it in place I never moved it again. I think this is very cruel."

"It is," I said, and thought it was also quite odd. "Was there anything about it that was unusual?"

"No. Nothing. I have some pictures that were taken when Sensei did the calligraphy. You can see it very well when he was measuring the paper and preparing to do the work. If you want I can show them to you."

"I would like to see them," I said.

She nodded and ate a bite of omelet. She'd ordered truffles and eggs saying that it was the season for the aromatic mushrooms. I had never tasted them and when I told the owner of the small restaurant about my lack of education he fluttered away and sent me a tiny dish with five slivers of truffle drizzled with olive oil and salt. It was different and delicious. I knew I'd never forget the flavor and even had a slight understanding why these small fungi could fetch the startling prices they command. I was eating quail breast on a bed of arugula with a balsamic reduction. It was delicious. Of course it was.

"Are the photographs on film or digital?" I asked.

"Digital."

"Could you send them to me?"

"Yes, sure. When I get home I will email them to your regular address."

I frowned. "Does the apartment have wifi?"

"We're in Nice, not Russia."

"Does that mean yes?"

She glared at me over her glass of wine. "Jean Claude is a very important person with his company and has to deal with people from all over the world, all the time. Of course he has wifi. He was very nice to let you stay in his apartment."

"Well, I was only there long enough to sleep last night and really didn't look around or even unpack."

She pouted.

I let her. One of the reasons that our relationship had not worked out is because I don't like to be manipulated and Kara doesn't like to let her control slip an inch. We didn't mesh for very long, but when we did, it had been very nice. She was doing the manipulating again and I didn't care. I wasn't bound to her in any way except as an employee, in the strictest sense of the word, and so I didn't give a rat's behind if her lower lip stuck out halfway to the boulevard.

She figured it out quickly, began to eat again and ignored me. I spoke up and asked Philippe if he planned on coming to the next day's classes. He nodded and motioned if he could join us.

"Sure, come on over." I didn't look at Kara.

He sat and talked about his work until we finished eating and I asked questions encouraging him. Kara was clearly annoyed with me, but not so that anyone watching would notice. Finally the waiter brought the bill and while we were settling it I was surprised by an abrupt exchange between Philippe and his sensei.

When they were done Kara stood and walked away. Philippe grinned and told me he was taking me to my apartment and that Sensei would see us in the morning.

"Don't you love French women?" he said.

"I don't know. They get a little annoyed when they don't get their way or you don't give them what they want."

"*Exactement*! So you must give them what they want and be happy with the result. Anything less will not make you happy in the long run." He smiled smugly.

I shrugged and motioned for him to lead the way. We walked several blocks through ancient winding alleys to his car and then he drove me around the small hill that separates Vieux Nice from the Port.

Jean Claude's apartment building is on the corner of the main roads Rue Arson and Blvd. Carnot and has a terrific view of the million dollar yachts at berth in the port. The first floor of every building near the Port consists of restaurants, bakeries, boulangeries, patisseries, or bars. I loved that. The apartment was on the third floor of the old building and even had an elevator, which I gladly used. I was suddenly exhausted from jet lag and the nonstop weight of being constantly on stage playing 'Sensei'.

The shower was large, the water hot, and the flow was strong. I was in heaven and when my head hit the pillow it was like closing a refrigerator door - total silence and the complete absence of light.

Chapter 5

I woke to the aroma of freshly baked bread. It was everywhere. My watch showed that it was still early, but I dressed and went down to the street and walked around the corner to the nearest bakery. There were two bakeries across the street from each other and I'd noticed at least two more within a block. The place was empty except for the proprietor and I nodded to her as she looked up.

"*Bonjour Madam,*" I said. In France it is customary to address the proprietor of a business when you walk in. Failure to do so marks you as a foreigner or a rube. It can also leave you waiting to be served for a long while. I am a fast study, though.

"*Bonjour Monsieur. Je peux vous aider?*"

I looked at the pastries, the breads, the cakes and assorted delicacies and thought, yes, you can certainly help me. I picked out a baguette, two croissant au beurre, a chocolate pastry that looked amazing and several other items that would probably get stale before I could possible get to them, but I was overwhelmed by the aroma and the rich colors and the display.

I handed her a bill large enough to cover everything and she gave me change. I only know a few hundred words in French and numbers just did not make the cut. It is easier to figure it all out later in the privacy of a quiet apartment than to stand in a busy store with frowning, impatient French housewives waiting for me to decipher the numbers. Some shop owners who are used to dealing with foreigners will simply write out the numbers and hand the piece of paper over to you. That's easy. 7.50 is the same in any language. A credit card is even simpler.

I walked past a street vendor selling coffee and bought a cup *au lait.* I drank it down in one swallow and ordered a double to take back to the apartment. I would have to see if Jean Claude had an American style coffee maker, because I was certain I would not be able to last on the tiny cups the French customarily linger over.

An hour later I heard the door bell and walked to the foyer to use the intercom.

"*Oui?*"

"Good morning, Sensei."

"Come on up." I buzzed the door and in a few minutes Philippe walked in carrying more pastries.

I led the way back out to the balcony overlooking Rue Arson and the Port. A yacht that had to be one hundred fifty feet long and three stories high was just docking. We admired it for a minute then turned away. Jean Claude had a Mr. Coffee and I was enjoying a cup with French cream and sugar and offered Philippe a cup.

"American coffee? Is this Sensei's, um, boyfriend's?"

I thought about that for a second. "Two things. First, it would be better to say, 'Does this belong to Sensei's boyfriend.' Otherwise you are stuck using a double possessive which is hard even when you are a native speaker. And two, Jean Claude is Kara's boyfriend?"

Philippe looked startled and then cagey.

"Well, you know these things…" he shrugged.

I didn't care. I was working here. I shrugged back. We stared at each other for a moment and then laughed. He said something in French and when I didn't respond he said, "It means, well, very roughly, better him than me…"

We laughed again. Men can be such pigs.

"We have a little while before we have to leave, unless you want to go look around."

"I haven't even seen much of the apartment yet," I said.

"It is a lot, I know…"

"And really, I'm here to teach Aikido."

"*Ah oui*, but you know there are things here, so close… like nowhere in the world."

I refrained from saying what came to mind.

"Every place in the world," I began, "has something unique."

"But where else in the world can you see history like this, and see the Mediterranean Sea… and still spend your nights in Monte Carlo with the most beautiful women in the world at your elbow, eh?"

"Well, I like history and beautiful women as much as the next guy, but the only gambling I do is to play a little roulette… I don't have a clue how to play baccarat in Monte Carlo."

"See?" he said and jumped up. He pointed at me and then the ceiling and then looked up. "Baccarat is as old fashioned as five card poker in Las Vegas. Everybody now wants to play this hold-them game from Texas where you finish quickly and then rush home… where you go 'whole in'." He grinned hugely. "History is right outside your door."

"I know," I sighed. Kara had preached to me for hours how ancient Europe and particularly France are compared to America, where a house a hundred years old was considered a national treasure. The house she'd grown up in was built in the eighth century. She'd labored this point so many times I quit listening. I got it. French people are very proud of their country. Imagine New Yorkers with good taste. Good grief.

"Do you?" Philippe insisted. "The principle game at Monte Carlo now is roulette. Would you like to go play? And did you know that we could walk to one of the greatest archeological digs in the world in less than five minutes? No?" He grinned hugely. "It is right there." He pointed.

I looked down the street and saw only an apartment or office building that sat off the main boulevard and had parking on the street level. I assumed that I had misunderstood him.

"No no, no… you can't dismiss this… um, Sensei. You know this is my world. I am Professor of Paleo-anthropology to the university and this is my museum. *Oui*?"

I did not want to alienate him or insult him. He was trying very hard to connect with me.

"I'm sorry Monsieur Professor, please explain about your work."

That stopped him.

"Ah, well…" That damned shrug again… "There was a dig. It happened a long time ago… That building, Palais Carnot on Terra Amata," he pointed. "The entire first floor is exactly the way it was when they called for Monsieur de Lumly to look at the old bones. You see, they were going to put up a building, apartments, and one of the workers saw some things that made him think it was important." He shrugged again. "They were beginning to dig the bottom, um, the cellar? No…"

"The basement," I said.

"Yes. And the worker saw things he knew were important, so he called Henry de Lumly. I was not here then, of course. I was still a child. They put in forty thousand hours of labor during the next five months. Can you imagine? And it was all volunteer labor. I came here because they have the museum."

"How old were the bones?" I asked. "Were they Cro-Magnon?"

"Oh, no! NO! They were four hundred thousand years old. They are from the time of Homo Erectus. Can you imagine? Homo Erectus in France so long before even Neanderthalensis? And there were no human bones... it was a settlement, with structures, cooking fires, bones from stag, elephant, bison... there were hearths for cooking and fossilized human waste. Do you see why this is so important? Can you imagine such a long distant cousin from the dawn of man, here, right here in Nice, before they gave birth to both Neanderthal and Homo Sapiens? Yes, they were our forefathers and this is an amazing site, an amazing look back in time to our first human kin. Do you see, Sensei?"

I looked down the street and then looked back at him. "Are you telling me they built the entire building over the archaeological site without disturbing it?"

"Yes! Well, the actual museum is a reconstruction displaying objects from several levels, but there is continued research on the many artifacts. I have developed photographic techniques that help identify and isolate important data on actual physical objects; information that until now has been undetected. I spend a lot of my time analyzing the original finds. "

"And they are still digging and examining it?"

"No, the dig is finished, but the examination of the remains and the cataloging still goes on. It is one of my duties with the university to oversee all this as a part time... you know this?"

"Yes, part time," I said.

He smiled a huge smile. "Yes, the graduate students do the cataloguing and I am in charge."

"Professor, I'd really like to see the dig."

"Sensei, *mais non*, please call me Philippe. I would love to show you my dig."

"Thank you." I said and offered him my hand.

"Bof, it is nothing. But we should probably go now." He stood and I went into the bedroom and gathered my clean gi and hakama. I realized that I had forgotten to check my email and then remembered the pictures that Kara was going to send to me.

"Philippe, do we have time for me to go online?"

"What do you think?" he said. "Will they start without the Sensei?"

I headed out the door. I hate it when people believe they are above others and make them wait. I would not do that to people who had spent good money and time to see me.

Chapter 6

The class was even larger than the day before, but it was Saturday, and that meant that students who would not or could not take time off work were finally here. There were also a number of people in the observation area both sitting and standing. It was crowded.

Seamus Murphy walked past and nodded to me. A tall, distinguished looking gentleman walked up as I was trying to weave my way to the office to change into my gi.

"Sensei?"

"Yes?"

"I visited your dojo several years ago and simply wanted to come over and say hello."

I looked at him and did recognize him, but could not put a name to his face. He was trim and handsome in that uniquely American way, and though quite old he looked to be in great shape.

"Warren," he said.

"That's right! The F.B.I. agent. How are you? What brings you to the Riviera?"

"Well, there's a big boat over in the Port of Nice that I came in on this morning, that's what brought me, but basically I'm just traveling around Europe this year and seeing the sights. I retired a long time ago. I was retired when I came over to visit you in Florida."

"Wait," I said. "I watched a ship dock this morning in Nice. A big ship, all blue and white, and it had a couple small runabouts that were hanging in berths off the stern. Is that yours?"

He laughed. "Not mine, it belongs to a lady I'm traveling with right now... Well, actually I guess I should say it belongs to her husband. These Europeans have a funny way about them..."

I looked at him and waved both hands in front of my chest and then shook my head. "Too much information..."

We both laughed.

"Are you going to get on the mat?"

"No, I don't have a gi with me. I just wanted to say hello."

"There's a store that sells martial art equipment two blocks away..." I was kidding with the old man, but his blue eyes brightened and he said. "Really?"

I nodded.

"Well, I may see you on the mat, then."

He hurried away and I turned to go into the office to change when someone touched me lightly on the arm.

"Sensei?"

I turned around again. A tiny woman was standing there and offering a camera. She said something in a foreign language which even I was able to grasp was not French. Still, I got the idea. I nodded and she quickly turned and gave the camera to a very hairy man who was not an inch taller than her. She quickly stepped over next to me, he snapped the picture and then she bowed and backed away.

The office was quiet, thankfully, but before I was even into my gi pants the door opened and Kara strutted in and threw several large packages onto her desk. I was nearly naked, but she didn't seem the least interested or embarrassed. I quickly suited up and was tying on my hakama when she looked up from a ledger.

"We are over the hill," she said.

"I may be, but I don't think you are…" I offered.

She seemed confused. I waited.

"We are past the bump."

I shrugged. I was starting to understand why so many French men do this.

"Oh, merde. We have sold enough to pay for your fee and airplane. Do you understand that?"

"Yes." I got it. I refrained from uttering half a dozen colloquialisms that sprang to mind. "For next weekend too?"

"*Oui*. So we might make some money to help keep the dojo open next year." This time she smiled at me. "If we have as good a crowd next week I will be…" She rubbed her thumb and two forefingers together. It didn't need to be translated. Aikido seminars are a business, after all. You need to make enough money to satisfy all costs but it's nice to make enough to pad the bank account a little, too.

"I have to go teach," I said.

She did not look up, just flicked her hand upwards at me motioning 'go, go…'.

I walked out onto the mat thinking I was glad I had not married her. Then, I was busy being Sensei and taught a good class. I focused on the nexus and centering and bringing the attacker into a controlled burn. Everywhere across the mat I saw eyes light up when someone would understand what I was teaching and I had to turn and smile at a blank wall on occasion as the light when on and someone really got it. For the rest of the morning and then later that evening and the next day as well, I gave as good as I got. Students had moments of clarity and understanding, or students were confused and merely going through the

35

movements. Students were having fun, being tough guys, strutting their egos, desperately striving, and some were just interested in doing Aikido somewhat differently than they did it at their home dojos. Yet some are always working hard for the next satori, the next great understanding.

Aikido is like this, always. We teach for those who are ready to understand the next lesson. It is usually the same things we always do, but it only happens when someone is ready for the knowledge. You cannot force feed a person this truth, they can only absorb it when ready, but it is always a wonderful thing for a teacher to be the one who leads someone to that moment and takes him or her through it.

They will think you are a genius forever because you were lucky enough to be the teacher standing in front of them when it happens. It is how reputations are made and preserved. People tell stories, and books are written about these moments of enlightenment, but it is always a matter of luck, and I have had an abundance of it. I have been blessed.

Chapter 7

Monday morning found me with a slight hangover staring at traffic grinding past on rain soaked streets. I hate morning rain. After the big dinner and party of Saturday night I had been ready for a little quiet time Sunday after the last class, but Kara's students had insisted on a dojo-only party that had been a celebration of all things French. There was way too much wine, too many homemade platters of delicious and varied food, guitars and mandolins and noise making devices of every description. And they danced

It's been years since I've seen people dancing with such abandon. And I guess I should also blame the deserts, Kara must have told her students my weakness for pastries and chocolate because it took up an entire table and I grazed freely. Too much good food and wine and dancing and more deserts... well, I've had worse hangovers from a lot less fun.

So as I looked out the window with an entire week of unscheduled freedom on the French Riviera before me, I decided to go back to bed. Then I thought of my computer and unchecked e-mails and messages, and decided to take my computer back to bed with me. The thought of coffee was powerful, though, and then I thought about sitting in a café with my laptop, a surly French waiter bringing me cup after cup of café au lait and me just watching the world go by. I could check out the internet in between watching lovely pairs of legs and ignoring haughty sneers. I got dressed.

The restaurant at the left of my door was not open and neither were the next two, but there was a nice boulangerie offering table service and lovely baked goods next door to them. I settled in and took out my laptop. The waiter wandered over amongst the empty tables. He moved toward me so slowly he might have been chatting with non-existent customers in his mind as he made his way over. It did not matter at all, because I had nothing better to do and I wanted to soak up all the culture I could while I was here.

"*Oui*?'

"*Café au lait et deux croissants s'il vous plaît,*" I said.

He sneered. It was perfect. I wanted to take a picture of him sneering, so I asked him if I could. Of course I don't speak French at all, mostly to order food or ask directions, so I had to ask him in English. I did it for a joke, something to amuse myself on a rainy Monday morning, but he surprised me. He laughed.

"Ah well, mate, it's a lot harder than you think, sneering. These bloody people have made it into an art form, they have. It's getting the attitude down correctly, now, isn't it?"

He said this in a sweet Irish brogue with a pleasant expression.

"I think you're the second Irish person I've met in the last three days," I said. "Except the first one is from Texas."

"There are a lot of us."

"So it would seem."

"There are more Irish in the world than any other nationality. You can check," he pointed to my computer.

"There are more Irish than Chinese?"

"There are more Irish dispersed in the cultures of other countries than any other. It's the great Diaspora, it is. The

Bloody British, potato famines, Van Gogh, and the ladies love us, you know. "

"Van Gogh?"

"The Potato Eaters? He spent a bit of time doing the pictures, you know. And U2, don't forget them…"

I laughed. "Can I have my coffee, now? And my two croissants?"

"Oui, Monsieur."

He moved off, but could not resist a backward glance with just enough Irish guile to make me laugh again. I turned on my computer and waited as it booted up. I was trying to get it to connect when he came back and slipped a piece of paper onto the table and mumbled, "This is the password for the wifi, it is. You'll be having a hard time without it." Then he moved off.

I was still waiting for my coffee when I saw that Kara had sent me an email, but then so had Monique and a dozen other people. I got busy. For the next hour I answered email, sipped coffee, nibbled pastry, and finally opened Kara's attachments. While they downloaded on the snail-like wifi signal I looked at Monique's message again.

Parker, you sweetheart, I don't know what in the world got into me when I saw you on the sidewalk. I'm really sorry if I acted like a complete fool, but I have been thinking about you so much lately and then there you were as if you had read my mind and were coming to carry me away. God, what an idiot. Well, it was wonderful to see you. Martin has a nice villa in Monaco and we are going to stay there next week before we go back to Africa. If you are still in France, and feel like a swim in either the pool or the sea, call me. I promise I won't attack you or make you so crazy you have to run away.

Love, Monique

Monaco. Where had I heard that name recently? Princess Grace, yeah, I knew that, Prince something… The waiter was walking past and I said, "Excuse me, can you answer a question for me?"

"Aye mate, my name is Sean, if you please."

I nodded. "Sean, what's special about Monaco? I've heard the name a couple times recently."

"Do you like to gamble? Monte Carlo is in Monaco."

That's what it was. Philippe mentioned it.

"Thank you Sean."

He nodded and walked away. It was still raining and I watched the foot traffic hurry past. Cars darted in and out of openings that Indy 500 drivers would have looked at with trepidation. Several world-class beauties wandered past. I watched it all, but was thinking about Monique.

If I was ever willing to be truthful, at least to myself, I would admit I regretted letting her get away. She was beautiful, passionate and wickedly smart, but more important we made each other laugh and there is nothing better in a sweet relationship than laughter. It is the grease that gets you through all the little problems that all relationships endure. Pure laughter is wonderful and she could get me laughing quicker and with more complete abandon than anyone I've ever known.

I wrote her back and told her to invite me over with a specific day and time and I would accept. I told her I was anxious to see her.

Kara's attachments had finished downloading and I elected to save them to my desktop. One by one I opened them and saw a simple progression of a group of people meeting and shaking hands or embracing. The next picture showed a small, old Japanese man looking at some brushes, light shining brightly over his shoulder so his face was almost lost in shadow. The next was a close up, taken over the man's shoulder of an old scroll rolled out on the table, the picture on the rice paper so badly faded it looked like mere smudges. This was followed by a shot of the old man measuring the rice paper of the faded picture that was glued, I assumed, to the split bamboo. The last two showed him painting the kangi for Aikido, three symbols, Ai, Ki and Do. And the final shot showed Kara holding the finished kakemono and standing next to Tamura Sensei. It looked very stiff and formal and I supposed it was.

I looked back through the pictures until I found the one taken over Tamura Sensei's shoulder. I expanded it. It was just a series of images that were little more than a blur. I saved a copy and then opened Photoshop and began to play with the images using different levels of sharpness, shadow, and color enhancements, but nothing really improved it. It was just an old faded image of nothing I could recognize. The finished kakemono looked very nice with the bright white rice paper and the hard blackness of the ink.

Sean asked me how long I would be visiting Nice and I looked up and told him another week.

"You'll come back again and have coffee before you leave, sure?"

"I don't see why not. I'm just staying on the corner."

"You have an apartment then?"

"Yes, on the third floor, at the front."

He looked at me quizzically and then smiled and nodded. As he walked away he turned and looked once again, but then was busy with customers and I felt as if I'd missed something.

My phone rang. It was Curtis.

"Parker."

"Hi Sensei. What's up?"

"Just having coffee and a croissant. Where have you been?"

"I, um, I've…"

"You hooked up with that dark haired lady. The blue belt?"

"Well, she has been very nice to me. It was a lot easier to stay in Villefranche Sur Mer than to go all the way back to Nice every night. I mean, I appreciated Jacques letting me stay with him, but if I have the choice to sleep in a nice, soft bed or on a hard couch…"

"Or to share it with a nice soft French woman…"

He laughed softly, clearly embarrassed. "You know Mariko and I are having trouble. We have ever since I got cut. I'm hoping some time apart will help us find some balance."

I didn't say anything, it wasn't any of my business, but I have a reputation for being very hard on my students when it comes to infidelity, especially when it comes to Aikido events. I haven't said anything to anyone in years, but a long time ago I released my senior student for cheating on his wife. It wasn't my business then, either, but I didn't think it made a good impression to have someone teaching for me who was not behaving himself. I know, I know… who's to say? Well, in that particular case, me.

"Curtis, I can't judge you. You have to make your own decisions. I don't know how I would feel if I had almost died from a cut like that. I don't have a clue. Just be careful. Are you going to be around this week? Do you want to do a little sightseeing?"

"It looks like I'm going to spend the week in Italy."

"Italy?"

"Yeah, Kathrin has a friend who rents an apartment in a village over near the Cinque Terre, those towns that are perched up on the bluffs above the Med? You walk from one to another and I hear it's supposed to be something you shouldn't miss."

"Okay, well, have a good time. Don't fall off any cliffs. Are you coming back for the seminar next weekend?"

"We're planning on it. I don't know why we wouldn't."

We? I waited.

"Okay, well I just wanted to see what was going on, Sensei."

"I'll talk to you later, Curtis." I switched the phone off.

The rain had stopped and I watched a large boat, a yacht, pull out of her berth and idle slowly out past the breakwater. I saw that a bill had been placed on the table and I dropped some coins on it then stood and started down the street. I went up to the apartment, but it seemed foreign and quite lonely all of a sudden. I must have subconsciously been planning to spend a lot of the week with Curtis. Well, I have never been bored and rarely lonely. I packed my laptop into its bag in the bookcase, found my camera, and headed back out.

I walked west and passed several more bakeries. There seemed to be one on every block. The building that housed *Le Musée de Terra Amata* was open, but there was not a soul in sight. I walked around the roped off site and wondered how anyone would have put it together that the odd bits of bone and rock sprinkled amidst the debris could be anything interesting or important at all. On the second level I slowly made my way around and studied each display, but unfortunately it was all in French and I had to rely on the similarities of words to help guide my curiosity. I went back downstairs and walked to the back of the large room and saw that there were offices and work rooms that held bins full of rock and fossils.

As I was turning to go I heard footsteps and looked up to see Philippe walk in carrying a large load of what appeared to be charts.

"Sensei!"

"Hello Professor."

"Do you like my dig?"

"Maybe, if I spoke French I'd like it a bit more, but it is fascinating."

"Then you are lucky to have a guide."

We spent the next hour slowly walking from display to display and Philippe explained the significance of everything to me as we went. It truly was fascinating, but after an hour my head was so filled with dates, and names of things I'd never heard of before that it was too much. He led me to a patisserie down the block and we sat and ordered coffee and pastry for me.

"What do you think, Sensei?"

"I'm overwhelmed."

He smiled. "We are fortunate that the Mediterranean Sea has such steep walls here. The rise and fall of sea levels during the last half million years has not reached so high as to disturb this find. Once the earth returns to normal it is possible that this, too, would be under water and be lost. Normal earth conditions are for sea levels to be about thirty meters higher than at present."

"What do you mean, normal?"

"When the Ice Age finally ends," he shrugged.

"I thought it had already ended."

He laughed. "*Mais non*, it is still with us. As long as there are glaciers and polar caps we are in an ice age."

"I thought that being in an ice age meant that sheets of ice cover the world."

He shook his head again. "A common misconception. As long as polar caps exist, it is by definition an ice age. For the vast, vast majority of the earth's existence there have been no polar caps. You know this? The earth is normally quite a bit warmer than it currently is."

This did not jibe with anything I had been reading concerning global warming, not at all. I looked carefully at him and asked him to explain.

"I don't know about man-made carbon making the planet warmer. It is not my field. I am a paleoanthropologist and have studied the rise of man over the last half million years as my prime field of interest. The planet has been going through a cool period for the last two and a half million years and it is marked by periods of glaciation. They are called periods of maximum glaciation. The last one ended about twelve thousand years ago and we are currently in an interglacial period. The time between periods of more cold… You see? The earth has been on a wild ride for the last couple of million years and it is my theory that it has been the periods of maximum glaciation coupled with the interglacial warm-ups that have been most responsible for man's evolution."

"But I thought we were worried about global warming?" I said.

"The earth will warm up, the oceans will rise, and the polar caps will melt whether man is here on the planet or not. It is the normal state of the earth. Ask any geologist."

"Then what's all the crisis management about?"

Philippe shook his head. Then he shrugged. "I suspect it has more to do with keeping the population distracted than anything. I don't know. I do know that nothing we do can stop it and I also know nothing we do can stop the next period of maximum glaciation."

"You mean there's going to be another ice age?" I asked.

"Well, as I said we are still in an ice age, but yes. There will almost certainly be another glacial period and I think we would be more wise to concern ourselves with preparing for that than worrying about ice sheets melting and opening up immense new opportunities for farmable land. There are many who seem to be so concerned about the warming and loss of a few unproductive islands that are in constant dread of tsunami and storms, but forget the millions of hectares of tundra and steppes that we will be able to convert to growing grains to feed the planet. Many people are foolish, but as I said, it is not my concern. Most geologists and paleogeologists, most intelligent people, in fact, are confused by all the misplaced concern."

I let that all soak in and realized that he had been speaking nearly perfect English. Well, it was his special field and most international conferences use English as the common language. It made sense. I said, "So you believe that the cooling and warming helped us become human?"

"Most paleoanthropologists believe it. It had to do with the radical climate changes that took place."

"It's weird hearing you say this," I said.'"From what I've been hearing you'd think climate change is new."

He laughed. "No, it has been swinging wildly since the cooling began, about two and a half million years ago. There have been tremendous swings in temperature that caused all sorts of radical, extreme changes; they are common and actually quite normal. And they happened far more quickly than once thought.

"Look Sensei, some people are chauvinists; they believe they are so special. The earth is like it is now, when they are here, so in their minds it must be the norm, because they are here to observe it. I think that is all. Arrogance and stupidity are the culprits here, not science.

"Well, that is quite humbling, but good to know. How does all that reflect on this dig?"

"See, the cooling and the ice sheets caused sea levels to drop by three hundred feet. The coast was many miles further south than it is now. Most of the planet's available moisture was locked up in glaciers and the whole inhabitable world was a terrible drought. Early humans wandered through here. There must have been many caves and places that are now under water that were rich with early history but are now gone.

"That is what I meant when I said we are lucky to have this site, because it is at the outside extreme edge of where the seas are during the current ice age. But it will be under water when the earth returns to normal and the polar caps are gone. Those glaciers caused horrible conditions in Europe and even in Africa. There was so little moisture that the planetary conditions were cold and dry to the point of worldwide drought. During the last period of maximum glaciation, beginning around thirty-five thousand years ago, Homo sapiens came very close to extinction. We almost did not make it."

Chapter 8

"How many different kinds of human species were there?" I asked as we walked back to the museum.

"I don't think we will ever know," he said. "We only recently discovered the Denisovan peoples. Yet my own DNA shows that I have about three percent of my genetic makeup from them. I am also about two percent Neanderthalensis."

I laughed.

"I am serious. Since we finished the homo sapiens genotyping we have learned so much you would not believe. We know when we started to wear clothing, we know that we interbred with our cousin hominids; we know when cattle were domesticated."

"Really? How?"

"We can look at the division of lines in other areas of the genomic code. For example, we know there are two types of lice, head lice and body lice. They are distinctly different by the way they cling to either hair follicles or fibers from clothing. We look at the DNA of the two types of lice and discover that they were exactly the same species once and diverged about eighty thousand years ago. Why? Because that is when Homo sapiens began to wear clothing. Why they started to wear skins of animals and devise clothing was probably due to climatic cooling and warming which might also be why they lost their body hair."

"Are you serious?"

"As a bottle of French wine," he said.

"What about cattle?"

"That one is fairly easy, because it is so recent. We analyzed the DNA from many people and discovered that people from northern Germany, Denmark and areas nearby all shared a common genetic attribute. They are all lactose tolerant. Comparing their DNA to others from the same area who are not lactose tolerant shows this deviation to have originated about six or seven thousand years ago. So you see, we know when people domesticated the cow and where it happened. DNA is a very useful tool. Have you had yours analyzed?"

"No," I said.

"Would you be interested in having it done?"

I thought about it. "Sure. How?"

"Come with me to the university this afternoon and we can do the cheek swab there. I will put you to the front of the line and it should be done by Friday. How does that sound?"

"Is there a cost?"

He looked wounded. You are my guest," he said. "I will simply ask that you fill out a questionnaire so we can enter your answers into the data base."

I nodded. It sounded fair.

"Sensei, you actually seem interested in this. Are you? You are not just amusing me? Being amused by me? You say this?"

"The term is humoring you. No, I am really interested in this."

"Then I may have something to show you that will change your life. We will see."

We drove to the university and Philippe walked me to an office where clinical types were all bent over microscopes or computer keyboards. Most were wearing lab coats. He turned me over to a pretty young woman and excused himself.

"I have classes for a few hours, but I can have one of these assistants take you back to your apartment."

"Not necessary," I said. "I would actually like to walk. It gives me an opportunity to see a part of Nice I otherwise wouldn't."

"As you wish," he said, then turned and entered a door with a small plaque that read 'Professeur Philippe Tessier'.

The lab assistant guided me through the cheek swab and then translated all the questions and my answers. It was nearly two in the afternoon by the time I walked out of the door of the lab and into a glorious warm Mediterranean afternoon. The sky was sapphire blue, there was a slight breeze and I walked slowly working my way downhill toward the bright sea in the distance. I knew all I had to do was get to the coast road and turn left. I would eventually end up at the port. Simple.

My phone rang. It was Monique.

"Hey Lady," I answered.

"Parker, you should have come to the Premier, it was amazing!"

I really couldn't imagine that.

"It was," she insisted.

I didn't say anything.

She started to giggle. "Okay, okay, it was awful, but the audience loved it and Thadenzuela were the king and queen of the night." This time she really laughed and I found myself laughing along with her.

"Can you come over for the day?"

"Which day?"

"How about tomorrow? I really want to see you."

"Tomorrow will be just fine," I said.

"Oh, that's wonderful. Martin is planning a big lunch, French style."

She gave me the address and told me how to get there and what time.

"See you tomorrow lover…"

There is was again, Bogart by way of Kathleen Turner. Tingles.

I put my phone in my pocket and looked around to see where I would go next. I was in an older, non-tourist part of town where working class apartments and small stores were close to the sidewalk and the street. Trusting my instincts I started downhill again and walked several blocks but came to a dead end that looked out over a wide flood plain that I could see was probably a run-off river for the Southern Alps.

This area is technically known as Alpes Maritime, and is not to be confused with Provence, which it is also a part of and which extends from the left bank of the lower Rhone River on the west to the Italian border on the east, and is bordered by the Mediterranean Sea on the south. I looked north and saw small mountains rising in the distance and knew that I was seeing the lower Alps. Apparently, I'd been confused by the sloping streets and mistaken the slope of the valley for the general slope of the foothills falling to the Sea.

I backtracked and eventually saw the Mediterranean Sea in the distance and changed course. Eventually the land leveled and I recognized a main road that led through a modern shopping district which borders the old quarter. I went in that direction and found a small café where I could rest and have a glass of chilled rosé.

My phone rang and I saw it was Kara.

"Bonjour. How are you?" I said.

"Hello Sensei. Where are you?"

"I'm in a café near Avenue Jean Medecin having a glass of wine. Where are you?"

"I am at the apartment of Jean Claude looking for you. Which café are you in? Are you alone?"

I looked around and then told her the name of the café and that it was across the street from Supermarche Casino.

"Wait there. I will come see you."

She left me listening to dead air. I really hate that. But a beautiful woman walked past then and looked me dead in the eye and smiled and I forgot all about the telephone. Several more lovelies wandered past chattering away like pretty women do the world over and I settled back and let the good life embrace my thoughts for a while.

The waiter brought me another glass of wine and I asked him for the menu. He told me they were not serving anything serious right then, it was between lunch and dinner, but he could bring me some light food. I nodded and he left. When he returned he had a platter of sliced meats, cheese, some breads and other assorted treats.

I realized I was hungry and ate while waiting for Kara. She had been all business bordering on surly. I wondered what I had done to cause this reaction. In her own words she had made enough money from just the first seminar to help keep the dojo on solid footing for a good while. I really wasn't too concerned, though, I have known her a long time and these kinds of reactions are exactly why I am not married to her.

She walked in twenty minutes later. It occurred to me that I could have walked from the apartment in that amount of time and wondered briefly if she had. She never gave me the chance to ask.

"Are you making progress?" she asked.

"On what?"

"On finding my kakemono!" She looked startled. "What have you been doing?"

"Sightseeing," I said with just the coolest inflection. "I also went to the University to have my DNA analyzed. I have been wondering if there might be a chance that I might be part Neanderthal. It seemed like a good idea. What have you been doing?"

Her face turned red and I saw her struggle to remain calm. She wasn't doing a good job of acting like an Aikido sensei at the moment.

"A Neanderthal, yes, this is what I thought. Why do you make jokes? You were supposed to find out who took my kakemono."

"Kara, I don't even speak French. Where did you ever get the idea that I might be able to find something that was stolen from you?"

"You are a detective and you looked at the lock and talked to my students. What were you doing? We did not even call the police."

"Philippe told me that the police wouldn't do anything and that it would be a waste of time." I tried to do the French shrug, but it felt stiff and she acted like she hadn't seen.

"That was before we discovered that the kakemono was missing. My kakemono..."

"Kara, listen to me. I don't speak French. How would I investigate? I wouldn't know where to start. I don't know the culture, and I haven't got a clue who might want something so personal..." I stopped.

"What?"

"What if it wasn't something personal?" I said.

"What do you mean?"

"What if whoever stole it wasn't stealing something personal from you but something that has a lot of value to someone else? What if the kakemono was valuable? I mean intrinsically valuable, like an antique or something. Where did you get it?"

"I told you I bought it at a sale at a house in Nice."

"Pretend you didn't and tell me again."

She pouted. There are times you want to kiss that pout for hours until it finally goes away and times you want to smack it right off her face, not that I ever would, but still... Finally she reached out and drained the wine in my glass and picked up a piece of bread.

"I bought it at a sale at a house in Nice."

"An art sale? An antique sale?"

"No! A sale of the property of the house."

"An estate sale?"

She blew air out in that way the French do that implies something smells bad or that they are disgusted.

"Yes. Someone had died... has died, you know?"

"Yes, go on."

"So they sell the things they had and that the children or wife do not want. Just certain things."

"Okay. Can you remember where it was?"

"*Mon Dieu.*" The pout returned and she looked out the window toward the street. The tram glided past on its rails and then stopped on the other side of the intersection. We watched scores of people climb on and off. Another tram slipped past going in the opposite direction. She finally turned back to me and said, "I have a piece of paper, a brochure. It has the details."

"Can I see it?"

"Yes, sure."

I sighed. "When?"

"Now." She stood up and I motioned to the waiter. He seemed amused. The whole conversation hadn't been all that funny, I thought, but left a tip anyway and followed Kara out and down the street. She'd driven and after she emptied the passenger side of all the accumulated debris, I squeezed into the tiny cramped seat. She rocketed off down the narrow street like a Le Mans driver in hot pursuit of a championship. I just closed my eyes and held on.

Chapter 9

She had to translate it for me, but what it said was that an estate sale was to take place on a given weekend and it listed a great deal of antique Japanese items, clothes and rugs.

"It is why I was interested. The Japanese things, you know... I thought if I could buy a sword, a katana... something authentic for the dojo. But it was far too expensive. All but the kakemono, and it was on a table with things like fans and little buttons."

"Netsuke?" I asked.

She looked blank.

"They're small buttons made from all sorts of things, ivory, exotic woods, and often carved."

"Yes, they were like that."

"Were they asking a lot for them?"

"No, just a few euros. Why?"

"Because, if they are old they might be very valuable."

"*Oui*?"

"Way," I said. What the hell, I thought it was funny. "Who was running the sale?"

"I don't understand." She sounded miffed.

"Who was selling off the estate? Did anyone say they were a relative or make any personal remarks that would lead you to believe that they actually had an interest in what happened to the things they were selling?"

"No, there was nothing like that. In fact, they all wore these same shirts so you could tell who was there to speak with and ask questions."

"So it was a company that comes in, prices everything, and then takes a cut of the total. Usually absentee owners do this so they don't have to be bothered getting rid of some dead relative's junk."

She didn't respond.

"So this person had a collection of Japanese items. Did you look at them?"

"Oh yes. The katanas and the... the sword furniture, the things that go on the sword... they were all very old and quite beautiful, but also very expensive. There was a suit of Samurai armor. It was complete and was decorated with gold and ivory accoutrements. It cost more than a new car. What else? There were some paintings of swans and mountains and there a lot of kangi that were beautifully framed. I think there were several rooms of oriental rugs and Chinese furniture, you know the old, heavy, carved kind... And there were a lot of personal things like clothes and shoes."

"What about kitchen things?"

"Why would you care about that?"

"Because if whoever authorized the sale wasn't selling off kitchen things, dishes or what not, it might mean that they were actually keeping the place and just wanted the personal stuff gone."

"Oh," she said.

"Well?"

"I'm thinking. No I don't believe I saw anything like that. There was no furniture for sale of a modern kind like you would actually have in a living room that looks out on the Mediterranean Sea, or lamps or foot stools and anything modern. It was all old."

"Can you take me there? I'd like to talk to the people who own the place and try to find out something about the man who died."

"Why would they talk to you?"

"Because if they don't, Kara, we're at a dead end. It's the only place I have to go and the only lead I have. Also it's always better to know something than not to know it. We need to find out where the collection came from and who the man was who owned it. We need to know if there was an inventory that might identify your kakemono and shed some light on its provenance. We need to find out if anyone might recently have come around looking for whoever bought the things that were sold. I'm a detective and I have a lot of questions to ask."

"So you think it might have been valuable?"

"Well, there are fans, and netsuke, and kakemono that are worth millions of dollars because of their age or because of who might have made them, or who might have owned them... And you said all those items were just thrown on a table. It could be that the company who liquidated the estate might have had a hole in their education and had not recognized what they were selling."

She looked surprised, which is something the French never do.

"Or they could have known and just stolen the majority of it. Or they couldn't identify it and didn't want to be bothered. Many questions. Let's go."

I stood and walked to the door.

Kara drove east and we wound our way up the peak that separates Nice from Villefranche Sur Mer. She navigated the switchbacks and narrow streets like a pro and soon parked on the edge of a road that wound along the summit of the hill.

I climbed out and stood staring at one of the most beautiful vistas I have ever seen. On my right, to the west, the city of Nice lay like a sun bleached woman languidly following the curve of the hills and the sea. To my left lay Villefranche Sur Mer tucked neatly into the compact harbor and climbing up the hills to the cresting cliffs. Before me stood a large villa and beyond was the Mediterranean Sea.

Kara had been speaking, but I was not listening. I just kept staring at the scene before me and shaking my head. It was stunning.

"What?" I said. "Kara, this is beautiful. Look around."

She blew air out again and said something about this is just a normal place for the Riviera and I was acting like an American tourist. She went over to the gate and pushed a button on the intercom. After a few moments she began to speak and I walked over to the side of the road and looked out over the bay before me. Ships were passing in the distance and the sun reflecting off the deep blue water was actually hard to look at. Even in October there were people on the beach and I saw tourists and shoppers wandering along the streets of the old town market.

"Parker!"

I looked up and Kara was holding the gate open. She motioned for me to come and I walked over and went through it into a large driveway. It was big enough to easily handle the three cars that were parked there. I watched an exquisite woman walk out of the door and pull a short robe on over her bathing suit. She tied a belt to keep it closed and then stood in the shadows of the overhanging bougainvillea and waited while we walked toward her.

Kara immediately began to speak and the two women began an animated conversation completely ignoring me. I had a chance to study the lady while she spoke to my friend and found myself totally captivated.

She was tiny, and looked Polynesian, with the slightest oriental cast to her eyes. She was full bodied despite a slender waist and her skin had an almost translucent quality while still being tanned. Her hair was black and suddenly she was staring at me with a slightly quizzical look on her face. She didn't seem to mind the fact that I'd been studying her though, and in fact seemed quite open.

"Do you speak English, by any chance?"

She looked startled but didn't say anything. After a full five-count she replied, "I don't very often. You startled me and my brain had to translate." Then she laughed.

Musical notes, that's what her laughter sounded like. I laughed along and caught a glare from Kara that would have frozen me to the spot while we were dating, but did not faze me a bit now.

"My name is Parker," I said.

"I am Anastasia Poullard. Friends call my Annie."

"Madam Poullard." I nodded to her and offered my hand. She took it.

"Please call me Annie. I insist."

"Thank you."

Kara started in again in French, but Annie turned and motioned for us to follow her through the door. We crossed a large, open room all done in white tile and warm wood and then followed her out onto the pool deck. She slipped out of the robe and lay on a chaise lounge, then put on a pair of sunglasses.

If anything, the view here was even better. The Mediterranean Sea seemed to float next to a railing that was all that separated us from the cliff's edge and the thousand foot fall to the sapphire water below. It was an illusion, I knew, because houses perched on the edge of the hill all the way up from the water. The designer and architect had built the house to appear to be the only dwelling in the world. It was an amazing view and a beautiful house. I told her as much.

"Yes, thank you. You can understand why my brother and I wanted so much to keep it when my grandfather died."

"So this house belonged to your grandfather," I began. "Can I assume that you are conversant with the things that were sold at the estate liquidation?"

"Of course, I saw his collection growing up. I was never very interested in it, however. My brother was far more fascinated by the whole samurai experience. I did love the dolls, the little geisha girls that he had in the display case in his bedroom. They were marvelous." She pronounced it the French way, *merveilleuses*. "When our parents were killed we spent a lot more time here than at home, but very soon we were both off to university and then working. I did not even have a chance to come home after Grandfather passed away."

"That must have been very difficult for you," I said.

"It was, but I could not leave the dig. There was just no way to trust anyone to do my work."

"Dig? Are you an archaeologist?"

"Oh, no." She laughed. "It's alright, I can see... a common mistake. No, I am an accountant. I work for the Musée National d'Histoire Naturelle in Paris. It is my job to keep our archeological projects on time and on budget. I was at a project in the Middle East. The paleoanthropologists and the workers... the supplies and support staff, it all costs money and everyone needs to be paid. There are numerous bribes and pay-offs and buying of stolen goods for exorbitant prices, but it all needs to be accounted for and handled. If I had left there would have been whole parts of the project that would have been shut down. The museum would never allow one of the project leaders to handle funds; it would have been war between the team leaders for who-gets-what allocations, so you see, I could not come back until the dig officially closed in September."

"This was a year ago?"

"Yes."

"Who handled the estate?"

"My brother Ken came home and arranged everything."

"Can you tell me where your grandfather came by such a large collection of oriental antiques?"

"He brought them here when he came from Japan in nineteen-fifty. He was Japanese; his name was Kenichi Mizushima. My brother was named after him but he goes by Ken."

She got up and went into the house. I looked at Kara, but she was not looking back.

"Are we learning anything?" I asked.

"Just that men are all fools for pretty women."

I laughed and she compressed her lips together.

"Seriously, are we finding anything out?"

She shrugged. A few minutes passed and Annie returned carrying a tray with a chilled bottle of rosé, glasses and some bowls of olives and cheese. There was a baguette that had been broken in half and several small plates.

"This looks wonderful, thank you." I said.

"Talking can be work. You see?"

"Yes." She filled a glass and handed it to me and I helped myself to the cheese and olives. Kara reached out and took the bread and broke off a rather large piece and settled back with it and a glass of the wine.

"So your grandfather was Japanese." I looked at her. She had taken the sunglasses off when she'd gone into the house and I smiled as I looked at her eyes. It was there, but only slightly. I'd been fooled by the closeness of the resemblance to a Polynesian woman I had known.

"I like it," I said.

She smiled hugely and then she laughed again.

"I do too."

"*Bof!*"

I swiveled around and looked at Kara. She glared at me. "Can we find out what we came for?" she said.

I turned back to Annie and asked, "He married a French woman?"

"*Oui*. Yes"

I thought for a moment. "Does your brother work close by? Is he available to speak with?"

"I am sorry, no. That is not possible. I might be able to find him, but it can take a few days sometimes."

"Excuse me?"

"I don't even know which continent he is on, or what city. He travels all over the world. He works for Saito; you know the international technology company? He travels all over with a team of engineers and fixes things. I don't really know what."

Kara interrupted, "Saito? Does he know Jean Claude Chastain? My... friend, *mon ami*..." The two women exchanged a look that I saw but did not understand. "He works for Saito and travels all the time too. I think he is the sales, you see?" She frowned and quit speaking English and said something in French.

Annie nodded and returned her blitz of French and then turned back to me. "My brother might know him, but engineers don't usually fraternize with the sales staff. Does he live in Nice?"

"Yes," I interrupted. "I'm staying in his apartment while he is away. I'm here teaching a seminar and trying to help my friend here figure out why someone would steal her wall hanging from her school. Her boyfriend is out of town."

The two women exchanged another look that ended with Annie looking at me with a curious expression. I forged ahead. "So you remember many of the items that were sold, but not in any great detail?"

"No, I'm sorry. As I said my Grandfather kept most of our family heirlooms in display cases."

"It must have been very difficult to have to sell off your family's most precious inheritance."

"Well," she made a show of looking around at the house and the sea. "We had a choice. We could have sold the villa. We both knew that there was not enough money to pay the tax or keep the place up without losing something. We could have kept the swords, but we would have had to keep them in our closets in our apartments. Selling them allowed us to keep the villa and always have a home here in Nice to visit when we want. We had to make a choice."

I nodded. It made sense. "So you are only visiting?"

"My brother and I each have a bedroom here and share the house when we are both here. Otherwise we stay here alone or in our apartments. Mine is in Paris. He lives in Frankfurt."

"Is there a manifest from the sale?"

She thought about it. "There must be. There had to be an accounting." She shrugged.

"Was there anything that was put up for sale that did not sell?"

"No. Not that I know of."

"Don't you find that odd?"

She looked steadily at me from over her glass. The blush of the wine matched her complexion in the fading light of the setting sun.

"My grandfather's things were of great age and value. It doesn't surprise me at all that everything was sold."

I turned to Kara. "How much did you pay for the kakemono?"

"Twenty euros."

I turned back to Annie and said, "That doesn't sound like much."

Annie turned to Kara and they spoke in French for a while. Finally Annie said, "I did not know about the table with the fans and netsuke. That should not have been. The netsukes were from a royal family and the collection should not have been broken up. The fans were all war fans from the fifteenth century and were also of royal vintage. My grandfather would never let anyone touch these things. This is very bad news. I will speak to my brother as soon as I can. I wonder if he knows about this."

"It would help us a great deal if we could see the manifest. They might have described or named the kakemono, so that we could at least know what was taken."

"I will ask him for it when I talk to him," she said.

The wine was gone, so I stood up. We had taken enough of her time and I figured we were unlikely to learn anything more without the sales manifest. Kara led the way to the door, but just as she was opening it Annie came out of another room and said, "Wait, when the liquidation company left there were cards everywhere. Here."

She handed me a business card, it said *Riviera Les Ventes de Liquidation* and an address. She took it from me and wrote her name and a telephone number and then signed it.

"Show them this and tell them they can call me if necessary and that I said it is okay to show you the list of items sold." She looked me in the eyes and said, "This is my personal telephone number."

"Thank you Annie, you have been far more helpful and gracious than two strangers had any right to expect. We are grateful."

She shook our hands and then we walked out into the darkening evening.

Chapter 10

When we were several blocks away Kara began to get nasty.

"Are you sure you want to leave?" she said.

"What?"

"Your little, sweet girl is all alone there. Don't you want to go back?"

"What are you talking about?"

"That woman!"

"Well, what about her?"

"She practically took her clothes off and climbed up you, on you... whatever!"

"Kara we interrupted her sunbathing. Hell, she could have been topless and that would have been completely normal for here, right? But she wasn't."

"And the way she begged you to call her..."

"She did no such thing!" I shouted. "Are you crazy? Even if she did it certainly isn't any of your business."

"Ooh, this is my personal phone number..."

"Oh, for heaven's sake, Kara..."

"And the way she showed herself to you when she served you her wine! Mon Dieu, She..."

"Kara, stop it." I said it quietly and forcefully. "We are friends. A long time ago we were more than friends but time has moved on. I don't know what you thought would happen when you invited me to come over here and teach, but we have not changed from the people that we were. It didn't work then; you can't control me. I'm sorry, but you just can't tell me what I can or cannot do. I'm going to try to help you find your missing property, but don't push me. I mean it. You are not responsible for me."

"While you are in France I am responsible for what you do," she hissed.

"I don't think so."

"Don't you dare take her to Jean Claude's apartment…"

"I'm never going to see her again."

"God, men are so stupid!"

She stopped at a red light and I climbed out. I walked around the car and stood there until she rolled her window down a bit.

"I'm going to walk from here. Tomorrow I'll go to the liquidators and find out what I can. The next time you see me you can treat me civilly or you can go to hell." I turned, crossed the street and walked away. I wasn't angry, I'd just been through this scene with her so many times before that I knew where it would end up, and how it would end up, and I didn't intend to go there.

I heard tires and turned to see that she had rolled her window all the way down and was laughing as she rolled past. I heard something that vaguely sounded like "Go to 'ell…" but her laughter didn't make it easy to figure out.

I stretched and walked back to the port and up the stairs to the apartment. I had been gone all day and the place was stuffy with all the windows closed, so I walked around and opened them. I poured a small glass from the open bottle of wine in the refrigerator and then took a shower. When I was dressed I walked into the kitchen for the wine and slowly completed the ritual of stuffing my fresh pockets with all the paraphernalia that men carry. I slipped my belt through loops and put my wallet in the back right-hand pocket of my pants. When the loose change and pen and comb were all stowed the only thing left was the business card.

I picked it up and looked at it. I would have to MapQuest it the next day to find the address. Then I thought about what I wanted to eat for dinner and where I wanted to go. There are so many great restaurants here. I turned the card over and saw the name and telephone number.

Was Kara right? Had she been offering me an invitation I had not even heard? Had she been interested in seeing me again? I know for a fact that men can be thick as a tree trunk and dumb as a fence post when it comes to women. I also know that I am far from attractive, half over the hill, a little too thick and a little too thin in all those respective spots. Why would she want to see me?

I figured the only way I'd ever know was to just ask her. I picked up my telephone and dialed the number.

Chapter 11

I was on my third cup of *Café au lait* the next morning when Sean stopped by and said, "You look like a horse that's been ridden hard and put away wet."

I laughed and said, "I haven't heard that expression since I was a kid in Wyoming."

"Ah, it came from Ireland, sure. You do look a bit worn thin though, mate."

"A long, pleasant night."

"And you wondered why there are so many Irishmen in France," he said as he strolled away.

"Not anymore," I muttered.

My telephone rang and I saw Philippe's name. I tried to remember if I'd made plans with him today, and when I couldn't I slid the line open.

"*Bonjour Mon Professeur.*"

"Ah, you are becoming a Frenchman in only three days! How wonderful. Have you had coffee?"

"I'm having it even as we speak."

"Where are you? Still at Jean Claude's apartment?"

"Practically. I'm sitting in a boulangerie just a few doors down."

"With a big red door?"

I looked around and saw the store front did indeed have a large red door.. "*Mais oui,*" I said.

"Wait."

I listened to the sound of silence on my end of the phone and then saw him walking down the sidewalk. He was carrying a briefcase and an umbrella and was dressed in a coat and tie. I thumbed off the connection and waved slightly. It was just enough to cause his attention to turn in my general direction and he saw me sitting at the back table under the awning. I was against the brick wall of the café with the ropes defining the restaurant area next to me. He did not return the wave, but veered into the café and I saw him talking to another waiter. They laughed and then Sean stopped and said something to him.

Sean listened and nodded and then walked out to serve another table outside on the sidewalk while Philippe walked over and joined me.

"You are causing the waiters to re-evaluate Americans."

"Why is that?"

"Because you act so French; you ignore them and treat them disrespectfully and tip poorly."

"Don't all Americans do that?" I asked slowly, trying to feel amused.

He laughed. "No, not anymore. Americans were so embarrassed by all the French and German and English people saying that you have no manners or that your parents were louts when they traveled to Europe that Americans do everything they can to ingratiate themselves. They even call waiters 'sir'! But you, you treat everyone like they are Aikido students and you are the sensei."

What the hell?

"Philippe, have I done something to offend you?"

"Oh, no, not at all, not me, but my sensei calls me three times in one night and does nothing but talk about how bad you are. She is my sensei, I wonder what is happening and then walk here and the first thing my friend talks about is you." He grinned widely and shook his head.

He glanced into the restaurant at the man setting up tables.

"I see."

Sean was clearing away some dishes from another table, but when he saw the look on my face he put the tray down and went inside. I saw him talk to the other waiter and then he was looking at me again and frowning. I picked up my coffee and took a sip. I took another and let the moment drag out.

"Philippe, are you having an affair with Kara," I asked.

He looked startled, but it quickly became amusement and he said. "No."

"Would you like to?"

He did the French air-blow between pursed lips. "She is my sensei," he said seriously. "She would make my Aikido very difficult if this happened."

I waited and then said, "I did. This was a number of years ago. It was in America."

We looked at each other then over our raised coffee cups and he put his down.

"Now it is my turn to see," he said. "Sensei, I apologize. She was very unpleasant, but did not ever mention that you had been… personal, with her. Now everything is clear. *Mon Deau*, you really are becoming like a Frenchman."

I looked at him flatly. Suddenly I just didn't care about the seminar, the kakemono, and certainly not about any damn Philippe. I thought about going home to my dogs and my dojo in Orlando.

"So were you coming here to defend her honor? Is that right? Were you going to drag me into the street and beat me? Have you suddenly become a master of La Savate and decided that you would give me a proper beating? Or were you just planning on being rude to me?"

Conflicting emotions crossed his face and I finally understood that for all his deferential attitude he certainly thought he was the better man. It was just so French and typical of academics everywhere. They think that being a teacher makes them a cut above. In Aikido it isn't uncommon either, but I have never been one to expect anyone to call me 'Sensei' off the mat unless we were at an Aikido function.

Many teachers do expect to be deferred to and have their students ingratiate themselves and even demand it, but I always thought that absurd. Of course it might be the only time and place anyone ever deferred to them in any way, so they really demand and want that kind of treatment. Men who might work in a factory or at some menial job become a teacher of Aikido and suddenly they expect to be revered like their Japanese masters. Sorry, I've never bought into it. I expect people to respect me only because I am the best man I can be.

He offered me his hand. I stared at him and after a long moment I took it and decided I was willing to let it go with him, but the restaurant and Sean really could go fly a kite. There are lots of restaurants and bakeries in Nice. I didn't need waiters talking about me to other customers.

I stood and threw a few euros on the table and walked away. Philippe caught up by the time I'd dug my keys out of my pocket and was unlocking the door to the apartment building.

"Sensei, wait."

"What is it, Professor?"

"Really, in France... I did not know. It makes a difference. You are a man and you rejected her. I see that. It makes sense and I did not know, only that she was angry. I was trying to make some sense of it and I handled it badly. How would you have done this? Please?"

I thought about it. All of the glow from the previous evening was gone and I just felt tired. He followed me into the foyer and then up the stairs to Jean Claude's door and then into the kitchen.

"I've done some pretty stupid things because a woman put me up to it." I said. "I've even gone up against some tough, mean bastard because he slapped a friend of mine around. But I've never been stupid enough to challenge somebody like me before. What were you thinking?" I said this and looked him in the eye.

We stared at each other and it dragged out and then we were laughing the way men do. We laughed and laughed and he slapped me on the shoulder and I nodded over and over. Finally we sat and it was alright. It was just too much late night for me and too much crazy woman for him. We were fine, now.

"I have something I'd like to show you."

"When?" I asked.

"Today, if you like."

"How long will it take?"

"Oh, it is a long way. It will take all day."

"Then no, I'm sorry. I have to go to this place to try and get the manifest for Kara's kakemono and then I have plans with a friend over in Monaco."

"Can I help?"

"Are you free?"

"Yes, sure. Except on Monday and Thursday afternoons I make my own schedule."

"I might need a translator," I said.

"And a driver?" His eyes twinkled.

"It wouldn't hurt, I said.

"But about this thing I wish to show you…"

"How about tomorrow?"

"I will pick you up early. Around ten."

"Ten is early?"

He shrugged and I went into the kitchen and made a pot of coffee.

Chapter 12

The estate liquidators were open and I could see movement inside as Philippe parked. We went in and Philippe asked for the manifest. It took ten minutes of discussion, rejection, argument and then a phone call to Annie to resolve everything, but finally we were sitting at a desk with a computer terminal.

"Do you speak English" I asked the young man."

He shook his head no, and then spoke to Philippe for at least five minutes.

"Sensei, he says that liquidation is a specialized way of selling and that their system operates on the principle that time is money. When they examined the estate they recognized that there were a number of things that would immediately go to dealers and they were called in. He says that the swords, the good swords, were bought by a dealer that has a shop here in Nice. All of the framed art went to a man in Marseille."

The young man printed out several pieces of paper and then displayed them to Philippe. He was treating me as if I were not there and I considered it rude but did not say anything. He was, after all, doing us a favor.

Philippe listened and then looked at the pages. He asked a couple questions and nodded again. Eventually he turned to me.

"Okay, here is the complete list. Everything that appears in blue ink was sold to private dealers prior to the sale. Everything in black was sold over the weekend that it was open to the public."

I looked at the list. All the items were listed using French words and the descriptions were also in French. This would take a while. The young man got up and walked away.

It was clear that the most valuable items had gone first to dealers. After a while I had it narrowed down to a handful of apparent antiques.

"Okay, Philippe, the highest priced item was this painting, *The Swans*. Then there are these two swords, then the two rugs...

I was making my own list and itemizing the big ticket items. A much older man came over and sat down heavily. We looked at him. He nodded.

"I own *Riviera Les Ventes de Liquidation* and I am impatient for you to leave so we can get back to our work. How can I help you?"

"I'd like the name and address of the man who bought these swords, also the framed art. Can you tell me anything about any of these items that you remember? Is there a system that you use?"

He called out to a young woman and she nodded and went to file cabinet." She will bring you the names. Now let me quickly run down the sale of this property as best I recall. The swords, there were three sets of both long swords and short swords with a matching device for holding them and displaying them. They were very old and very valuable as you can see by the sale price."

The three sets had sold for thirty thousand euros each. The framed art had brought an even one hundred thousand.

Two of the oriental rugs had gone for twenty-five thousand each.

"They were worth a great deal," I said.

"They are worth far more than they brought, but when you work with dealers you must factor in the notion that they are in business to make money. Just as we are. We could easily have sold these items for twice and even three times as much, but it would have taken ten times as long and we are not in the business of selling antiques or art, we are in the business of liquidation. If someone wants to just get rid of their belongings then we help them.

"The rugs were silk from Hereke, Turkey, the finest in the world. They were silk and six hundred knots to the inch. An Italian dealer came over from Florence to get them. He stole them at that price, but it was the best offer we had. The same is true for the framed art. There were several old sumi-e that were very nice but we simply bundled it all to Francis for one hundred even. The swan sumi-e might fetch a half million at auction."

"Then why did you sell it for such a low price?" I asked.

"Because the auction house will take thirty percent and the dealer must double his money and perhaps it only sells the three-fifty? Are you a business man? It was a fair price, but not a great one."

I thought about it and nodded. I saw what he was driving at.

"So when the dealers had come and gone we were left with the rest. I had a team of three at the house for twelve hours each day. We sold everything and there is the accounting." He pointed at the pages on the table.

I looked at the pages and asked, "Why were the netsuke and fans and the kakemono sold as afterthoughts? They were very valuable."

"To whom?"

"To a lot of people I would think."

"We brought in our dealers, and they are experts, believe me, and no one offered a franc for them. What can I do? I offered them and finally one woman bought all the buttons and a fierce looking young man bought the fans. The other wall hangings, the kakemono as you call them, were just throw away items. The same is actually true for the poor man's personal items: his shoes, clothing, that sort of thing. We sell a fine old suit for practically nothing to get rid of it. The Chinese furniture would have sold for a fortune ten years ago, but today you can't give it away. It is the whim of fashion."

Philippe spoke to him in French for a moment and then sat back in his chair.

The older man continued. "Most of the Japanese items were genuine antiques, but there are few dealers who specialize in this area here in Provence. In Paris we would have done much, much better, but the time of year that we held the sale is our busiest and we simply could not take the time to bundle and hope for a greater profit in another market. The seller made over three hundred thousand euros total and that is a very good liquidation."

"How much of a cut do you take?" I asked.

He stood and walked away. The young woman brought me a piece of paper that had the information we were promised. She handed it to me and did not smile.

"Au revoir," she said.

We left, but merely sat in the car. I was contemplating my next move. There only seemed to be one.

"Can we find this dealer do you think?" I asked.

Philippe took the paper and read the address. He shrugged and started the car. After driving a few block he did a u-turn in front of a large truck and after the ensuing fist shaking and name calling he parked in front of a store front that even I could recognize as an antique store.

We walked in and I said hello to the proprietor, as is proper. He said hello and asked if he could help us. Philippe took over and explained that we wanted to ask about the swords and the samurai items.

"They are all gone, *Monsieur*. All but the suit of armor, would you like to see it?"

I nodded and he walked us into a back room. It was assembled and displayed on a mannequin of some type and I had to admit it was very impressive.

I explained that we were trying to establish a provenance for an item bought at the sale and hoped that identifying the other items might aid us. Philippe said that this was similar to establishing the age of a stone tool, for example, by carbon dating the bones lying next to the tool.

"All of the items sold had the family crest. Well, most of them did," he said.

"Did you identify it?"

"Oh, yes, certainly. When you come upon a find like this – a family treasure of heirlooms - you always try to contact the heirs first. They often will pay far more than market value in order to restore their heritage. I established that it was from the Yamada family of Edo. They were an ancient clan and very close to the Imperial family."

"Did they buy the swords?"

"Unfortunately no. The last member of the family died in the early nineteen sixties. Apparently he himself had fallen on hard times after the Second World War. There was simply no one to contact. Here let me show you."

He led us to a wall dominated by a large book case. After examining several covers he chose one and carried it over to an enormous oval table half covered with all manner of items. "Here," he said.

I looked at the book while he pointed to a crest. He then carried the book into the back room and walked up next to the suit of armor. He held the book up high so we could examine the crest on the helmet with the one in the book. Even from five feet away it was easy to see that they were identical.

"The last of the Yamadas maintained the family heritage of service to the Emperor," he said. He was an admiral of the Japanese Imperial Fleet and apparently was actually at the surrender. That is really all I could find out about him."

"Thank you for all this," I said. "Can you tell me if you have ever heard of a painting called The Swans?"

"Swans are a common theme in Japanese sumi-e painting," he said as he carried the big book back to the shelves. He reached up and then brought another big coffee table sized book back to the table. He looked in the back at the index and then flipped pages until he came to what he was looking for.

"See? These are all good examples of swans in sumi-e paintings."

I looked and saw a number of pictures of paintings and even a sculpture with swans as the theme. I told him about the picture that had gone to the dealer in Marseilles.

"I remember it. It was not large, but it was exquisitely done. I even thought about buying it, but the price was too steep for me. I had all that my resources could bare to purchase the sword and armor collection."

I glanced at Philippe. "Anything else?"

He shrugged.

"Thank you, sir, you have been very kind to show us these thing and to talk with us."

He smiled and walked us to the door.

Chapter 13

Looking at my watch caused Philippe to ask if I was late.

"Not yet," I said. "Monique said lunch and to be there around 12:30."

While we waited at a light a few blocks from the Port I asked him, "What have we learned?"

"Nothing."

"'Well, that's not entirely true," I said. "Somehow the Yamada family heirlooms found their way to Nice. The old man, well, as a young man, showed up here with hundreds of thousands of dollars worth of ancient Japanese treasure."

"Hardly a treasure, I would think," said Philippe.

"Forget what the liquidator said. He was concealing a lot of sales information. We only have his word for the actual prices paid, and I think the rather cavalier way he dismissed something as well known and valuable as the netsukes and war fans and the kakemono was just too telling. No, I think that estate was actually a treasure. Okay, maybe not on a par with Versailles or the Louvre, but it wasn't chump change, either."

"Chump change?"

"It means pocket change, coins."

"Ahh…"

"Anyway, we know that Kenichi Mizushima arrived after the war with this stash of ancient goodies and who knows what else. What does that tell us?"

Philippe frowned. "We are trying to logically analyze all the facts that we know and extrapolate conclusions? How delightful. You are Hercule Poirot, Sensei."

"Great. Look, he was either a member of the Yamada family and brought his inheritance with him, or he stole it, or somehow got it from someone that stole it. Right?" I glanced over at my driver.

Philippe frowned and pulled the car over to the curb in front of my building. "The dealer said that Admiral Yamada was the last of his line and that he fell on hard times. But he also said that he did not die until the next decade. Would he willingly give away his estate to a junior relative and watch him take it away from Japan only to live meagerly until he died? It doesn't sound very Japanese to me."

"It doesn't sound very human, to me." I growled.

"So it was stolen." Philippe said this with absolute French conviction.

"Probably. But by whom? By Kenichi Mizushima? I need more information. But here is the important thing. Every piece of that estate, every piece that was brought over here was valuable. There were no 'valuable to who?' pieces. That was pure crap on the part of the liquidator. I know he made a lot more from the sale than he has listed there. Sure there was the accumulated junk of just living here in France, but the Japanese things all were valuable.

"Okay, I see that. We can accept the premise..."

"So what was so special about a faded, ratty, old kakemono that they merely tossed on the sales table? Why was it special to Mizushima? Why did someone go through all the trouble to smuggle it out of Japan, and then keep it in a glass case squirreled away for fifty years?"

"I think you have a point, Sensei Poirot," he teased.

"Great. I'll see you tomorrow if you still want to take me to your secret locations and show me your special surprise."

I grinned at him and he grinned back. Whatever had happened earlier had opened something up between us and I thought we might end up being friends.

"I will see you early tomorrow," he said.

"Yeah." I waved and walked away. "Early around ten."

He gunned the motor and I heard his tires squeal as he pulled out into the vicious traffic of the coastal road.

I walked up to the apartment and changed into a nice jacket and tie. As I was getting ready to leave I noticed something that did not seem to fit. My briefcase, a large leather shoulder bag reminiscent of an old mail bag, but outfitted with many compartments for a laptop, files, pens, credit cards and what have you, was not on the shelf where I left it. It was in exactly the same spot but one shelf higher. The shoulder strap was even crossed and tucked the way I always do, but it was not where I could merely lift the flap over and see into it.

I pulled it down and looked through the many compartments. Everything seemed to be there. My passport, money clip, pens, phone cord and charger… everything was where it belonged. I opened the laptop and thumbed it on. It's set to my fingerprint as the password. Unless you have my finger, it isn't coming on.

The last attempt to open it had occurred just over an hour ago. It had to have been Kara. She had a key to the place. I was suddenly quite angry and alarmed. I must have upset her far more than I assumed when we visited Annie and I'd chosen to walk back. I knew I had to call her and clear the air, but I realized I was running late and French trains do not wait for you.

I sat on the upper deck and watched the towns of the Blue Coast ramble past. In twenty-five minutes I was in Monaco. The train station seems to have been carved out of a sheer rock cliff and when you walk out the back way you descend hundreds of steps down past an ancient stone church and come out across a busy street from the port. The bus stop is right there and I waited for five minutes before one arrived heading up the hill.

Monique had said it didn't matter which bus I took because they all go the same route until they are past the road leading up to Martin's villa. It was close enough to walk but I was still feeling tired and out of sorts from the long night I'd had. I stood as the bus drove up the hill and rounded past the palace, then followed the coast a few blocks to the front of the large square in front of the Casino at Monte Carlo. I stepped off. Martin's villa was supposed to be about six blocks straight up and a little to the East. It took me thirty minutes of wrong turns and missed signs before I was standing in front of the wrought iron gate and thumbing on the intercom.

"Oui?"

"Parker," I growled.

"Oui."

I waited and in a moment I heard footsteps coming across the gravel on the inside. The gate swung open and Harvey Green pulled me inside and gave me a huge bear hug. I'm not the kind of man who hugs other men. I rarely hug strange women, either. It just isn't me, but I slapped Harvey on the back to let him know I was alive and he let me go and then turned and led me back toward the villa. The place was eerily like the villa that had belonged to Kenichi Mizushima with nearly the identical layout. Once inside, however the similarities ended. You could put Mizushima's entire villa inside Martin's great room. The famous director met me halfway across the room and offered his hand.

"Parker, great to see you. Glad you could come. Hope you're hungry."

"Thanks Martin, I'm glad I could make it too. And I am hungry."

"We're having a traditional French lunch with about eight courses and at least that many wines, I think," Monique said as she walked up and put her arm around my waist and kissed me on the cheek.

"I can't wait," I said.

"No need to," Martin said and waved toward the main hallway. "Follow me."

We walked past a branching hallway that Monique said was the guest wing. "I think there are at least six bedrooms. I have a lovely suite that opens right out onto the pool with a private bath."

Martin led us past a kitchen and then into a formal dining room that looked out over the blue Mediterranean Sea. Of course it did. Actually, after a moment I realized that the entire wall was window and there were no obstructions to the view. Unless you happened to be seated with your back to it, that is. I also noticed that I was becoming inured to the view. Kara had been right.

Already seated were Thad Deep and his wife Valenzuela, known collectively to all the tabloids as Thadenzuela. On the end Martin assumed the master's seat and at the far end sat Harvey. I was directly to Martin's left and Monique next to me. Peppered between us all were several beautiful young women who were chattering and giggling. Martin's daughters?

I sat forward and offered my hand to the one directly across from me. "I'm Parker. How do you do?"

She looked at me with such lascivious directness that I was taken aback.

"These three are Martin's guests," Monique said quietly, motioning with her chin. "He always treats himself after he finishes a movie. Ignore them."

I glanced quickly at Martin who was giving directions to a man in waiter's garb. Martin appeared to be about sixty and was in good shape. He was clearly wealthy and in a league that I couldn't even hazard to guess. Three? Whatever floats his boat, I thought.

A glass of champagne appeared in front of me and after a moment Martin cleared his throat and we all looked at him. He was holding his glass and I saw everyone else was doing the same.

"I'm making a toast and giving formal thanks to the man who singlehandedly saved *Above the Fray*. Parker, that movie would have died along with Deep if you hadn't put your own body between him and that damned sword. Bravest thing any of us have ever seen. We owe you now and will always owe you."

"Here, here…" chimed in Thad Deep. Valenzuela looked dreamily away and set her glass down.

Monique squeezed my leg. Harvey tossed off the entire glass and nodded at me, meeting my eye mano-a-mano.

I was embarrassed. I thought about all that Curtis had suffered when he tried to stop the assassin first and had been cut from shoulder to waist. He had nearly died.

"Here's to Curtis," I quietly said and held up my glass. They all murmured assent.

"Let's eat!" roared Harvey and it finally dawned on me that Harvey was half drunk.

I laughed and said, "I'll drink to that." and drained my glass.

Baguettes appeared on the table along with bottles of sauce, vinaigrettes, and olive oil. As I was reaching for the bread a waiter slipped a small dish in front of me. I knew instantly what it was, the classic omelet that celebrates white truffle season. The chef had even sculpted a small rose out of shaved slivers of the amazing mushroom. It had been drizzled with olive oil and sea salt and sat directly in the middle of the mound of eggs.

Another glass of wine appeared in the place of the champagne. I lifted a sliver of white truffle and ate is slowly and let the woody, earthen taste fill my nose and mouth. The wine held a taste of flint and sweet old oak and matched the dish so perfectly that the two became instantly inseparable in my mind. I ate and drank slowly as did all the adults at the table. The three young women chattered on, but it was pleasant and not annoying as it easily could have been.

One dish followed the next and the French chef demonstrated why the finest food and wine in the world is the cornerstone of the culture and its single greatest accomplishment. Voices relaxed, smiles grew soft and intimate or gentle with unrestrained satisfaction and happiness. The wine worked its magic and by the time the duck breast was brought to the table, seared and thinly sliced with the simplest of balsamic reductions drizzled over the still sizzling fat, I was practically in a stupor.

Another glass of wine appeared but I waited until the taste of the duck was nearly gone before I sipped it. I sat upright. I tasted it again and then became aware of Martin watching me.

"Like it, Parker?" he said.

"You understand I am not a wine expert, or even a real admirer, right? I really haven't got a sophisticated pallet."

"Parker, do you like it?"

"I think it is the finest wine I've ever tasted. Powerful, subtle, more flavor packed into a single sip than I have ever imagined possible, yet... I don't know how to say it..."

"I think you said it pretty good," thundered a happy Harvey from the end of the table.

"Yes, not bad," nodded Martin Scarlotti.

"What is it, if I may ask?"

The waiter turned and then presented me with the bottle. I read, Domaine Romanée Conti La Tache, 2005. I'd heard of the great burgundy before, most people know it as DRC, but had never tasted one and now I knew what the fuss was all about.

"Now I can actually feel as if I've properly thanked you." Martin smiled at me and nodded with his chin at the bottle.

Everyone turned to the duck and the wine and eventually the waiters were taking away dishes and bringing cheese plates and offering salad.

"Parker, while you're around I want you to feel like you can come by anytime. It doesn't have to be a formal meal, just come by for a swim."

I reached out and shook his hand. "Thank you Martin, I wasn't expecting anything like this. What a meal."

"We eat like this all the time," laughed Harvey.

Monique giggled. "We actually do. We always have meals like this. At least we always do when we've finished a major movie, premiered it at the Cannes Film Festival, and happen to be in the south of France... in October!"

Everyone laughed at that, even the chippies. Monique's comedy timing is impeccable and I've sometimes thought she could read a phone book and have people laughing until they cried.

Martin stood and we all joined him.

"Stick around, Parker, have some cheese and coffee. Have a glass of Sauterne; I have a really nice Château d'Yquem over there. We need to go talk to a man about a movie. Oh, there is something else. I'm hosting a small dinner party at Monte Carlo Friday night. It will start around eleven in the dining room. If you feel like coming I'll put your name on the list and we'll expect you. Do you like to gamble?

"I like roulette."

"Then you should fit right in. Wonderful. Come early for cocktails and we'll ride over together."

Somehow Harvey looked as sober as a judge and everyone in the entourage filed out and I could hear doors opening and closing and finally I was left alone with Monique and a dozen cooks, waiters and chefs.

We walked to the pool and sat on lounge chairs. I was practically immobile and couldn't imagine how Martin and Harvey could actually go somewhere and do business.

"Parker, I have a question I need to ask."

I reached over and took her hand. "The answer would be yes, sweetheart."

"Oh, good. You do have a tuxedo."

"What?"

"Parker, do you have a tux with you or not?"

"Good grief, no." I thought about it. "Actually, I don't have one anymore. My last one was ripped to pieces. I need to get one. Christmas and New Year are always busy for bodyguards."

"Ripped to pieces?"

I nodded.

"How in the world did that happen?"

"Justin Bieber filmed a special at Disney and then did a private concert, black tie, for all the big shots. I got stuck with the personal protection on Bieber, he's another one of those nuts that doesn't like guns. It was all supposed to be a big secret, but when I escorted him to the waiting limo there were a thousand thirteen year old girls trying to get to him."

"And they ripped your tux?"

"Ripped? No, they shredded it. It was the worst mob scene I've ever been in."

"I thought you swore you would never do personal protection again."

I sighed. "Money only goes so far…"

"Albert should buy you another tux."

"Oh, that's no problem. He gives all his top men a good allowance for first class clothes. He wants his men to be dressed as well as the big shots they guard. He says its important and cheap considering the good will and image."

"So do you want to go buy one?"

"I thought maybe a little nap might be nice…" I looked into her eyes as I said this.

She got it.

"No. We need to get you some clothes. Let's go."

"Okay, fine." I stood. I was actually relieved.

"Where? Oscar has a place right down by the casino. So does Ralph and Giorgio…"

"Oh, well, let's not keep them waiting." Sarcasm was lost on her, she was on a mission and shopping was its name.

"I think, definitely Armani."

"Hey, Monique, I work in these clothes, let's not get crazy."

"Whatever…" She waved her hands back and forth and I knew that what I wanted wouldn't amount to much.

The walk helped clear my head and settle my stomach. By the time I'd been measured, explained why I needed the tux to be a little more loosely fitting through the shoulders than is customary, chosen the midnight blue – under harsh light black looked sickly, chosen a lighter wool than normal – I live in Florida after all - picked out accessories, paid, and agreed to pick it all up Friday afternoon, the day had grown dark.

I walked Monique back to the villa and when I expected her to walk through the security gate she turned and kissed me on the cheek and told me she was looking forward to Friday. Then she walked through the gate and let it close behind her. I was on the outside, suddenly, looking in.

Chapter 14

It was after ten by the time I reached the apartment. I knew I needed to call Annie and make arrangements to see her and discuss what she knew about her Grandfather's early years. I was beat though, and went to bed.

The next morning found me looking for a new breakfast restaurant. I settled on a small bakery that had a couple petite tables on the sidewalk. The coffee was better and the croissants were the same. It was cheaper.

Annie answered after a number of rings and I realized that it might be too early to call, but she seemed happy to hear from me and after a few moments of small talk agreed to see me for a late dinner.

"Um…"

"Yes?"

"Well, I like to cook and think you might like to come here for dinner."

Oh yes. "Thank you, I would like that very much. I have plans to be out of town today, but have been assured I will be back before dinner. I'll try to have my friend drop me at your villa."

"Oh, that would be wonderful. Come any time."

"Annie, before you go, just a question…"

"Yes?"

"Can you tell me where you were overseeing the dig? I'm spending the day with a paleoanthropologist and that kind of thing, to say I know someone like you, it will give me something to add to the conversation."

She laughed. "Yes, sure. It was in the foothills of the Zagros Mountains in Iran. We were excavating a village which some of the faculty believed was one of the oldest sites ever found that included agriculture. They found grains and tools, artifacts that seemed to conclusively demonstrate that the people had been farming. It was dated back to almost 12,000 years. Nothing like this has ever been found so far east in the Fertile Crescent."

"You know, I find I am really fascinated by this subject. I would like to hear more tonight."

"*Au revoir, Chéri.*"

"I'll see you later." I thumbed it off and finished my coffee.

Philippe called twenty minutes later and told me to dress casually, to wear jeans if I had them or chinos. I was waiting for him on the curb as he rolled up to the corner and jumped in as soon as he came to a stop.

"You are ready for an adventure," he said with a grin. "This is good. I see you are anxious."

"You bet. Let's go. Where are we going?"

"We will drive to a village where I grew up and then go to a small farm I have purchased. It is in the Provence countryside and you will find it beautiful."

He did a u-turn in the middle of the intersection and oncoming traffic joined the following cars in honking their horns, shaking fists and shouting obscenities. He didn't seem to notice.

We drove out of Nice and after passing through the heart of Cannes turned north toward Grasse and away from the Côte d'Azur. We talked about his interest, the ascent of man, and I was able to contribute my bit about Annie. He seemed delighted and wanted to know all about it. We were getting along easy and he asked me about my Aikido career. That led to a series of discussions on several topics. After a couple hours that featured smaller and smaller roads and tighter and narrower bends and switchbacks we entered a small village.

"This is Volonne. I grew up here. My father was a school teacher and my mother ran the post office."

I looked around and saw a small French village just like all the other small French villages we had passed along the way. "Other than the fact that you grew up here is there anything special about it? There must be or you wouldn't have driven all this way to show it to me."

He grinned. "This way." He drove off at a far more reserved clip than usual and we wound our way along the bluffs that overlooked the river. He took at least three turns onto smaller dirt roads and then we followed a paved two lane blacktop for perhaps a mile and then back onto more dirt roads. Eventually he pulled into a small path that led through a copse of trees and then followed a pasture fence until it ended at a ramshackle farm house.

"We arrive," he said. He climbed out and walked over to the farm house. The door was not locked and he strode right in and I followed. It was a wreck. Debris was scattered on the floor and the walls were mildewed and in some places the plaster was actually falling onto the cracked tiles. Broken furniture was piled in what had been the dining room.

"What do you think?"

I walked back outside and looked the place over with the thought of restoration. It was a disaster. "Unless there is some really serious, historic reason or maybe something about taxes… Philippe, I'd tear it down."

He laughed and his teeth were white in the sunlight. "Good, you are an honest man. Come with me."

We walked behind the house and across a small yard to a barn. Behind the barn was a small building that resembled a garage like so many seen in the United States. It had a heavy door and I could see no windows. The building looked like it had been dug into the hillside and its entire rear seemed to be a part of the cliff.

"This is why we have come. Now I must tell you my story." He placed a backpack on the ground and took out two bottles of beer. He opened them and offered one to me. It was warm, but you can't always get what you want. I drank.

"When I was a boy my mother would sometimes bring mail to the farmers who had a hard time getting to the post office. It wasn't something she did all the time, and I have always suspected that the jars of honey, the hard sausage, and the big loaves of country bread that they would insist she take for thanks was as much a part of her driving out here as her proclaimed altruism. She often insisted I join her and although I was a boy and wanted to be playing by the river and looking for fossils and fishing, I came.

"One day she visited this farm and while she was inside talking with the farm wife I watched the old man carry a bundle of garbage over to a hole in the ground right at the base of this cliff." He pointed toward the rear of the garage. "I was astounded. The bundle dropped into the ground and disappeared. Every time my mother came out here I asked her to let me come and later when I was old enough to drive I would visit the old couple, do some chores, and look at the mysterious hole.

"When I entered the university and decided I wished to study archeology and later specialize in paleoanthropology I thought about this farm. Having degrees in both fields allowed me access to several of the most preciously guarded sites in France and I noticed many similarities between existing caves and this location. There is a reliable technique that involves testing for wind or breezes emanating from a fissure or opening in a cliff face. I could detect such a breeze coming from the hole in the ground here.

"Anyway, I was home for Christmas a number of years ago and my father told me that the old couple had passed away, first the old farmer and then a few weeks later the old woman.

"I made inquiries. There was only one heir and after a short negotiation I purchased the site quite cheaply. The farm produced little and it is so far out of the way, you see? Then I prepared. I brought ropes and equipment to build a scaffold with an electric winch. I brought lights and a generator. Unknown to them, the university loaned me a small fortune in equipment for exploring caves and tunnels and when it was all assembled I made my first entrance into the Caves of Volonne.

"Parker, imagine what it was like! I had a heavy scaffold with three hundred feet of wire that could lift 800 kilos. I suspended myself and slowly lowered myself into the earth. At first it was just a hole, black and ugly with debris and rot. Then my light disappeared. Ahead of me was a large cavern. I pushed away from the wall behind me and stepped up into the entrance like I was stepping into a ballroom. The floor in front of me was littered with bones. I turned and looked back at the chute and turned my light downward and saw, perhaps one hundred feet below an enormous pile of debris. Even from so far away I could see the skeletons of mammoth and saber toothed cats."

I stood mesmerized as he was telling me this story and found myself looking at the garage. "It's there?" I pointed.

"*Oui*. But wait, there's more. When I went into the cave at first I believed it was just a... How do you say it, like a foyer? But at the end it narrowed and then I found myself walking, bent over for a few steps, and then into a cavern the likes of which no scientist has ever seen. And it was untouched. It was pristine. It is still perfect and it is the only one of its kind. And you are the only other person to ever have the privilege of seeing it. Come."

He walked to the door and took out a key. The door was strong, heavy and secured with several heavy duty locks. He pulled it open and then went inside. I stood in the doorway, but hesitated; it was black as night in there. I heard a grinding noise and then the sounds of a generator, a small diesel, and suddenly lights burst bright. Philippe stood next to a platform that was dug into and anchored by the hillside. From the platform a set of steps descended steeply into the earth. There were heavy ropes for a stair rail and I saw that light was shining up from below the opening. He held out his hand and offered me the first descent.

"Why don't you go first and show me how it's done?"

"As you wish."

I watched him turn and face the stairs like a ladder and then he disappeared down into the cave. I followed and found the cave entrance large and well lit with light bulbs in fixtures suspended from cables carefully anchored into the cave wall. An electric line snaked carefully around the cable. I saw it went to the back of the cavern and then through a crack in the back wall. Philippe had placed a wooden platform a few inches above the packed earthen floor. It was about a meter wide and solid. I followed him back and through the crack in the wall and bent over, moving slowly through the narrow passage.

Daniel Linden

When I was able to stand up he was directly in front of me and I waited. After a moment he stepped to the side and my heart stopped in my chest. Twenty feet in front of me, painted on a flat stone cave wall probably fifteen feet tall, was the most perfect painting of a wooly mammoth I have ever seen. It looked so life-like, and the colors were so vivid it left me speechless. I could only stare. It felt as if I could step forward and stroke the long fur or climb up onto the tusks. It felt as if it would turn any moment and see me hiding here.

Lights were placed so that it was illuminated completely with very little shadow. I saw that the lights wound down through the cavern and that the boardwalk followed the path of the cable. "There's more?" I whispered.

Philippe nodded and led the way. The path turned to the left and I saw immediately to the right of the mammoth there were three dire wolves snarling over what appeared to be some kind of deer. They were ripping it to pieces and the detail would have done any modern painter proud. The colors were real, the blood red, and the dire wolves' fangs yellow. High up the wall there were some kind of birds soaring over the feast, probably vultures. The figures changed every few paces. It was a menagerie of the early human's world, of all the things that he saw and the animals that sustained him and moved him. I walked slowly down the boardwalk until I came to the place where that wall ended in an abrupt fissure. The very last figure depicted was a woman crouched over something. She held a baby to her breast. She was as human as any young woman today.

Emotions swirled inside my chest and I have never wanted anything more in my life than to reach out and to touch this masterwork that had been created a thousand lifetimes ago by an unknown painter. I then realized that I was weeping, tears flowed down my face and I heard the smallest hitch and realized that Philippe was standing next to me and that he, too, had tears falling down his cheeks.

"It happens every time," he said, and wiped his eyes with a handkerchief. "It is like the whole of the human race is here. All our pain, all our triumphs, all of the things that everyone wants and needs and dreams of... Here in this small woman and the man who loved her enough to give her immortality. Do you see the way she holds the child? Do you see that there is pain there and tenderness? Every time I look I see more detail and understand both the artist and the woman better. It is as if I can see back in time and can actually live here with the Cro-Magnon and watch their lives unfold all on this huge stone cave wall."

I went back to the first painting and stared at it long and hard committing it to memory. I repeated this with every painting in the gallery. Finally I saw that Philippe waited for me at the far end and I walked slowly to him.

"You have made the find of a lifetime."

"Yes, I have, perhaps many lifetimes. And who knows what they will find when they excavate the dirt below our feet. Perhaps the artist lies here or perhaps his woman or their child. Who knows? I have never gone down to the pit. I know it will take teams of men a hundred years to carefully catalog everything there."

"But you're going to do it aren't you?"

"Oh no. I leave this to experts who do this special kind of work. It will have to be done in special lighting with special glasses. Too much light, this kind," he pointed at the lights above. "This kind of light will be used rarely. It would destroy the colors. No, I intend to give the cave, the land, the buildings to the French people. I will donate it entirely to the Musée National d'Histoire Naturelle and the government. I will only ask that it be named the Tessier Cave of Volonne. I am not without vanity. Are you ready to see the rest or have you reached capacity?"

"There's more?" This time I was really startled.

"Sensei, the best is yet to come. There is something here so special, so fantastic that no one will believe it. It will be argued and discussed for generations. Books will be written and men will fight over this, but it is here and it is fact."

Chapter 15

He moved down the boardwalk past the crouching woman and bent to pick up an extension cord.

"These paintings are much, much older. I have dated this first gallery, the work of Cro-Magnons, or early modern humans at 33,000 years with carbon dating from the pigment that has fallen to the cave floor from the actual painting. I am certain it is perfectly accurate.

"This next gallery is perhaps 70,000 years old and as such provides mankind with the first glimpse of true art from what must surely be Homo sapien neanderthalensis. If it is not him then it could only be Homo erectus and if that is the case then we are standing in a treasure the entire world will know about. Homo sapiens came out of Africa approximately 70,000 years ago and did not reach the Iberian Peninsula until around 40,000 years ago. It had to have been done by Neanderthals. I used uranium-thorium testing techniques to establish the date and it predates any other find, even the El Castillo Cave, by 30,000 years. Sensei this is the art of Neanderthals.

He plugged in the cord and the gallery lit up with harsh figure drawings and ocher hand prints. The floor dipped and began to decline steeply and I could not go far into the gallery. It was clearly much older. A thin sliver of accumulated moisture shone on the rock face, but after a moment I realized that it was not moisture but a covering of accumulated stone. In the same way that stalactites build stalagmites this rock had gradually coated the artist's renderings.

"You see how the paintings are covered by a frosting of mineral deposits? This is the greatest thing a cave can have because it takes many tens of thousands of years to accumulate like this. There can be no hint of forgery or deceit. This is…" Philippe's voice failed him. "This will rock the academic world to its core."

I nodded. "How long have you been exploring this cave?"

"About ten years. It has taken me that long to invent the photographic technique that I have been seeking. I knew it would be possible once computers became fast enough and once digital cameras were perfected and the right software was written. I have had to wait, but now I have documented the entire cave. I have photographed every inch in huge gigapixel formats with the finest lens and equipment. I have used only the purest tungsten light for the exposures and now I am in the process of creating photographs that will actually show these paintings as they were when they were created. That is enough."

He walked back and waited for me to join him and when I neared he pulled the plug and doused the lights in the Neanderthal gallery. We walked toward the narrow crevice and when I turned around he smiled sadly and said, "It is time here, as well."

We climbed up and out of the cave. Philippe waited until I was outside then turned off the generator and followed me out. The day seemed incredibly cool and bright after the darkness and cloying closeness of the cave. He locked the deadbolts on the heavy door and we drove away.

We returned to town and he pulled to the curb in front of a small restaurant. When we walked into the treasure trove of aromas I felt my stomach growl with hunger and anticipation. It had been a long time since breakfast. The proprietor came out of the kitchen and hugged Philippe. He waved his hand at the room and we took a table in front of a large window overlooking the town square.

"Sensei, this is Maurice. He owns this restaurant."

I nodded and said hello. He spoke for a few minutes with Philippe and then left. A few moments later he returned with a baguette and a bowl of olives and an enameled pitcher filled with cold pink wine. He poured generous glasses and then left.

I tried mine. It was slightly sweet and very crisp. I smiled and drank some more then reached for the olives.

"How do you like it?"

I nodded and then spent ten minutes telling him about the incredible meal I'd had the day before. When I was done he just shrugged.

"It is a French Sunday dinner. No more."

"Well, the wines were over the top," I said.

"Yes, that is money, you know. You drink what you can afford. If money is no issue you drink the Grand Cru and if it is an issue you drink what is best from what you can afford. This wine," he indicated the pitcher in front of us covered in condensation. "This wine is perfect for our meal today and nothing you drank at your famous director's house could possibly compare."

"What are we having? I didn't see a menu."

Today Maurice has made cassoulet. For this wonderful dish we have the best wine in the world."

"What is his specialty?"

"Everything Maurice makes is special."

"But is there a theme for this restaurant?"

He shook his head. "Sensei, this is the true French restaurant, forget what you see in the old quarter, this is the magic of French cooking. Every chef in Nice would kill to have what Maurice has here."

"Okay, Philippe, imagine I'm completely ignorant of such things. Imagine that I'm just an American sitting here with no education at all. Explain it to me."

Sarcasm was not lost on him.

"Okay, Sensei, I will explain why this is normal and special at the same time." His eyes twinkled. "The olives you eat are from a small farm about twenty miles from here that is owned by Maurice's brother. He is the only provider of these *Provençal* olives. The meat that will be in our cassoulet is from the farm of his father. The wine is made by a neighbor and has never touched the inside of a bottle; it is made and delivered in oak casks and is served from them. The herbs that will flavor the cassoulet are grown in back of the restaurant. The beans are from the local market and were grown locally. Maurice would never think of making his famous cassoulet unless every ingredient was perfect, ready to be used, and from a place he personally knows.

"This is French country cooking and it is what the great chefs try to emulate, but never perfect. The simple truth is that each day Maurice goes about and sees what there is available. Then he decides what he can make from the ingredients that are fresh, ripe and available. He only prepares dishes that are made from what there is. He has no 'menu' and if he did he would tear it up the first time he would have to use something imported from far away or something that had been frozen or came out of a can. That is why no chef in Paris can compare to him."

I have to admit I was impressed and it made perfect sense. Maurice came out of the kitchen door with a casserole dish and set it on the table between us. He went back into the kitchen and returned with two large bowls and then served us. The cassoulet was incredibly rich and steaming with sausage, chunks of pork, ham, and large, luscious white beans. The gravy was thick with herbs and tiny bits of browned meat. I tasted it.

Philippe was right. The flavor was unlike anything I've ever had, not just from the unique blend of herbs, spices and ingredients, but from the vitality and freshness of the ingredients. I ate forkful after forkful and had to stop myself from simply shoveling it in. It was delicious.

"What do you think? Is it as good as the food at your dinner yesterday?"

"Delicious," I said, and then returned to the bowl.

He waited and then sighed. "You know, everything in that dish was still at a farm yesterday."

I nodded and kept eating.

"You really can't compare this kind of food with something prepared in Nice."

I nodded again and drank some wine and then returned to the cassoulet. Bread was a perfect complement, crusty and still warm from the oven; I used it to sop up the gravy.

"There are many who never get to eat something this marvelous."

A loud voice called from the kitchen and spoke a few sharp sentences. Philippe laughed and picked up his fork.

"What was that?" I asked.

"Maurice just told me to shut up and eat and leave you alone so that you can enjoy the meal."

I was surprised and it must have shown.

"Oh, it is alright. He is my uncle and has taken a rod to me often enough when I was a child to still think he can order me around."

"He's your uncle?"

"*Oui.*"

I laughed and kept eating.

When we were finished we lingered over the last of the wine. I asked him what he had been talking about when he described the photography.

"Ah," he said and sat up. He held a finger in the air. "This is good that you should ask. I will tell you."

I realized that I was now seeing Professor Tessier.

"I spent over a year carefully photographing the walls. Not every day, you understand, but when I felt I could take the time and do it correctly. Eventually I had it all, but the colors were inconsistent and there were many places - it was done 33,000 years ago – that were faded and mute. At first I tried Photoshop to enhance and return the colors to their original intensity. The size of the files I was using was huge and consequently the computer was overburdened and very slow. My first attempt took twenty-six hours to complete a simple command to 'sharpen'."

"What size files were you using?"

"The University had done much work with Kodak in the last part of the century and they were by far the leaders in technological applications for digital cameras. I was taking files that were more than six gigabytes of areas of the wall no greater than twenty by twenty centimeters. I was using Nikon and Canon lenses at first, but Kodak provided me with several hand ground lenses that were priceless. The University was curious, of course, but it cost them nothing and I always had a standard approach on a recent dig to demonstrate my usage.

"The breakthrough came when one of my students saw some of the work I had done on another dig and suggested he could write a program that would enhance the images without altering them – exactly what I wanted – so I offered him a teaching assistant position to compensate him for his time and he has been working on it for six years now. It is finished and it is amazing."

"Why? If it isn't too technical, that is."

"No. It is simplicity. It takes the photograph and removes each and every pixel. It analyses the pixel, every last attribute, and then it stores the information. Once the photograph has been broken down it then looks at all the pixels in a general area surrounding each and every other surrounding individual pixel and then notes all the similarities. Once that is done it creates a database for all the areas of similarity and for all the areas of contrast and then begins to reassemble the photograph building up or tearing down the properties of the individual pixel in relation to the surrounding pixels."

I must have been staring at him stupidly because he stopped.

"It brings out all the hidden attributes and reconstructs the photograph to the object's original condition. It does. Trust me, I have hundreds of completed pictures of the cave and you will not believe it."

"I'm impressed once again, Professor."

"You will see. You should come to the University Friday and I will show you the book..." he blanched.

"Oops?" I said.

He stared at me. "No one is to know..."

"You're publishing a book on the cave?"

"Sensei, it is a secret, well not in the strictest sense, many people know about it, but not where the cave is or even that it is a secret... They are publishers, not scientists. And I desperately need the money. I sank every franc I have earned for years into making this project... how do you say... prosperous? No, to pay? I will give it away, but I must try to recoup my loss, so I plan to make the announcement, take a team of archeologists and paleoanthropologists to the cave, show them, have a press conference where will I present the cave to the Musee and the French People, and then announce the publication of the book. I have said that I am not without vanity and if I am going to give a priceless piece of history to the world and my country I should at least receive a little something in return, no?"

"At the very least," I said.

"We are only waiting until the computer at the lab finishes the last of the photographic images. All the text and the story have been completed and the editing is done. Even the book cover and all, it will be very fine, I assure you, and it will be a tribute to France."

"It will be filthy lucre."

He stared at me and then burst out laughing. "You are becoming a Frenchman!"

I offered my hand. "Congratulations Philippe, you have given the world an amazing gift and the country should reward you handsomely, but I expect that even in your beloved France the truth is that no good deed goes unpunished. I think publishing in conjunction with the announcement is brilliant."

"And it will insure that no matter how much each and every bureaucrat in the Musée, and in the Department of the Interior, and in the Parliament, and the President's office wants to have the cave named after him, it will always be the Tessier Caves of Volonne."

It was my turn to laugh. It was brilliant. "I hope I can get a copy autographed by the author."

"It will be my honor." He thought for a moment. "Can you come to the University Friday? Your DNA results will be in and we can look at them and I will show you the galley proofs of the book."

"I'd love it, but it will have to be in the morning."

"That is perfect."

Chapter 16

Philippe dropped me off at the top of the hill between Villefranche Sur Mer and Nice where the driveway and the side road split. Annie met me halfway across the walkway after buzzing me in and she threw her arms around me and kissed me with a playful happiness.

"*Mon Chéri*," she whispered, and then giggled. "Have you had a long, hard day?"

I couldn't help it. I hugged her and then swept her off her feet and carried her to the house. She was so tiny and happy, like a doll that was made for a man.

"I have had an amazing day. One of the great days of my life, but I can't tell you about it because it would be a conflict of interest."

"Oh, that sounds like a challenge."

"It isn't meant to be, but still, it was a fascinating day."

"I am happy for you. Every day should be a challenge and a mystery and better than the day before." She smiled at me with real joy and I couldn't help but respond.

"Would you like a glass of wine?"

"Yes," I said and walked through the living room and out onto the pool deck. A table had been set and there were several lovely plates sitting on a bed of ice.

"I love pâté," I said.

She smiled at me, but said nothing.

"Did I make a mistake?"

"Cheri, you cannot make a mistake, you are not French. You are not expected to understand."

"Okay, what did I say?"

"You said *pâté*. This is *un bloc de foie gras de canard*. It is a slice of duck liver, prepared by *moi*, for a very sweet man. *Pâté* can be anything... like sausage, or your ground meat or... hot dogs? Duck liver is more, much more..." She leaned over and sliced a generous piece off the mound and put it on my plate. She reached into a small bowl and picked up a few granules of salt and slowly sprinkled them across the pâté, then she gestured.

I tried it. It was creamy, unctuous, and more subtle and yet more bold than anything I had ever tasted with the name of liver. She handed me a glass of wine and I took a sip and sat bolt upright.

She laughed out loud.

"What is this?"

She showed me the bottle and it took a few minutes to recognize. I was expecting a French appellation, but what I was looking at was a chardonnay from California, from the vintners at David Bruce. "Good grief," I said.

She came around the table and settled into my lap and took the wine from my hand. She took a sip that lasted so long I would have sworn that she was draining the glass, but when she put it on the table it was hardly diminished. We took our time, sampled the delights, enjoyed the scents, the textures, and the moon rising over the Mediterranean Sea; we nibbled and sipped and tasted all of the possibilities and promises and then finally went back to the food waiting on the table.

"How would you describe it?" she asked.

"Unctuous. No doubt about it."

"*Oui, onctueux,*" she murmured. "That is it exactly. I will have to quiz you on all the things we share." She smiled up into my eyes and then got up and went into the kitchen. She returned with a plate of vegetables: radishes, carrots, sliced cucumbers. "*Crudités,*" she said, and placed it between us.

We had a really wonderful dinner. It was simple, and elegant just like her. Anastasia Poullard was a real beauty and very refined as well as sophisticated, but she was also a born prankster and a ton of fun to be with. She teased and toyed with me all the while we ate and then sat close to me afterward while I watched the waves of the Mediterranean Sea roll into the shore. We laughed until we were leaning into each other from tiredness and the longer I sat with her the more I felt comfortable in a way I thought I never would again. Finally she turned away from me, slipped her legs under and then turned back. She had a wry grin, but underneath there was something older, sadder, and wearier than I thought her pretty face could show.

"So Parker, what is it you wish to know? I can tell when a man wants something. And since the one thing that most men want you will surely have, and as much, and as long, and as often as you wish... tell me please?"

I nodded. "It's about Kenichi Mizushima, your grandfather. I need to know everything about him. Please just tell me what you know; anything might be a clue in this matter."

"So you are still detecting? Still looking for the wall hanging that looks like nothing but smears? Okay, I will tell what I know. It isn't really very much. I was born in Paris and other than the times my family traveled to Marseilles for the Spring Carnival I rarely saw him."

"Marseilles? I thought he lived here?"

"When he first emigrated from Nippon, Japan, he settled in Marseilles. It is a seaport to the west of here."

"I know of it, vaguely," I said.

"Yes, well, he came in the very early nineteen-fifties and settled there and started a business."

"What kind?"

"I don't really know. Shipping, maybe? Some kind of import or export? He was my grandfather and you know how it is with children. Grandpapa, where is my gift? Where is my new toy? What did you bring me? Always about the child, you see. I never remember asking him, 'How is business, Grandfather?'." She said this in a low masculine voice and we both smiled. "Is this not how children act, even in America?"

I thought about my Grandpa Spenser and wondered if I had ever asked him about his business. I knew he was a retired locksmith, and that he still worked at it part time when an absolute expert was needed to solve a thorny problem for a bank or a business that none of the local experts could handle, but actually asking him about it? I couldn't remember ever having done that. Most of our conversations were about where we might put the eel pots or the crab traps, or if the bass would be on the beds yet. Fishing, hunting, boats and motors, those are the kinds of things I was interested in when I visited him in Florida.

"I think you are correct," I said. "So how did he move here and build this villa?"

She glanced around and shrugged. "Hardly a villa. But it is very nice and now with the market… maybe. He did it, that's all I know. When my parents were killed he came to Paris and spoke at length with my *grand-mère et grand-père Poullard.* We stayed with them until we went to University

115

and spent our vacations between both *Grand-Père* Mizushima, and my father's family in Paris.

"He was retired by this time, so I don't really know what his business might have been or if he was still involved with it or anyone in a business fashion."

"Does the name Yamada mean anything to you?"

She frowned. "No, not any more than any name…"

"Did he leave anything other than the villa and the belongings in it? Were there any stocks or bonds or business ownerships… anything that could tie him back to Japan?"

"No…"

"Not to get too personal, but was there a great deal of cash?"

"My brother took care of all that, but no, I don't believe there was."

"Then how was he paying for all this?" I waved my hand around the room.

She frowned and slowly sat upright. She glanced out at the sea and then back at me. "There might have been a pension?"

"If he was self-employed, owned his own business, he would have had to privately fund it. Where is that fund?"

"I don't know…"

"Because it seems to me…" I took a deep breath. "It seems to me that something doesn't add up. Something smells fishy here. Something about the whole deal is wrong."

She stood and went inside and a few minutes later came out with a folder.

"This is everything I have on my grandfather's estate. Why don't we go through it and see what there is to see? I am now very curious, myself, and since I cannot ask my brother, Ken, I would like to know as much as I can."

"All right..." I reached for the folder and she clicked a light on next to the sofa.

We spent the next hour looking through the life of a man of serious mystery. It seemed as if he had sprung up whole cloth at the age of 75 when he commissioned a house to be built in the town of Villefranche Sur Mer, right on the border next to Nice. He had a few slips of paper that seemed to reference Marseilles, but nothing at all about a pension, a bank account, a safe-deposit box, a business, anything at all that could have provided him with the means to survive in an environment that even the most jaded had to call the life of the rich and famous.

"What does it take to keep the villa, here?" I asked. "In terms of taxes and insurance, the basic water and electricity..."

She thought about it for a moment and then got up and left the room. When she came back she had another folder and sat down with it pressed against her breast.

"This is from Ken's desk," she said. "We can see."

After doing the math from receipts and records I nodded to myself. "So without too much effort, from the sale of the personal effects your grandfather left you, you have enough to keep the villa for about ten years. This figure here, this is it. That is not counting any investment proceeds or increase in expenses. That is just one-for-one dollars against debt."

"Euros," she said.

"Exactly." I nodded and thought. "This is the bare bones number. Transportation, or maintaining a vehicle, food, clothing... he had a lot of nice clothes, I understand, an evening out or entertaining friends... So what was he living on?"

"I don't know."

"Unless he was quietly selling off the pieces he had brought from Japan. Unless he was just selling something every so often when he started to need more funds, like selling off retirement stocks." I looked at her for a long moment and then asked the question I had been dreading.

"Where did he get all this stuff? According to what I have been able to find out, it all belonged to a family named Yamada. The family was of royal lineage and the last remaining member was an admiral in the Japanese Navy that surrendered in Tokyo Harbor in 1945. According to my sources, he died practically penniless in the early sixties. Is it possible that your grandfather was actually a member of the Yamada clan and that he smuggled all the family treasure out to keep it from being seized or destroyed by the Allies? Is it possible that you are a Japanese princess?" I hoped I wasn't laying it on to thick; that by putting a little sugar on it I could mitigate the ugliness of the accusation that her beloved grandfather was a thief.

She sat looking at the file folder in her lap. She sat quietly for a long time. Every so often she shook her head back and forth and then she silently closed the folder, reassembled the first one, and stood and carried them out of the room.

Way to kill a beautiful evening, I thought. Accuse her grandfather of being a thief. Still, despite what it might cost, it's better to know than not to know. I sat there a few minutes longer and then decided to let myself out.

When I stood I saw her in shadow in the darkened kitchen. She stood there silently. I walked slowly toward her and saw she was no longer wearing anything. Without clothing she seemed diminished, tiny. As I walked toward her, though, and began to recognize her beauty, she seemed to grow larger and more powerful. Taking my hand she led me into the bedroom where she seemed to engulf me and overpower me while she turned into a whirlwind, and finally, I felt exhaustion and warmth and peace and then let the time and the long day and the love carry me to a deepness of sleep I have seldom ever known.

At some point I woke in the night to see her standing in the moonlight before the opened veranda doors. Ice blue light reflected from her hair, and the way she looked into the sky, her upturned chin, the soft curve or her figure mesmerized me. I wondered if I was dreaming such beauty and if not, what I had done to deserve it.

Chapter 17

When I walked into Jean Claude's apartment I connected my phone to its charger and waited for five minutes before picking it up and thumbing it on.

"Call Opie Taylor," I said.

The miracle of the modern telephone, reaching out and finding connections to people all over the planet always amazes me. I was born long enough ago that there were no cell phones and when I first started using the darned things I was shocked and I still find them fascinating. You used to have to know where people were to call them.

"Hey Parker, what's going on?"

"I am embroiled in a mystery and need your help. That's what's going on. First though, how are you? What's up?"

"Oh, not much, really. Fat Albert took on more than he can chew with a new Saudi Prince. He guaranteed around-the-clock protection for him and his entourage before he knew that the dumb shit has about 75 people traveling with him and they all want to feel important and have a personal bodyguard. That's about 50 more guards than Albert has on retainer, so he's busy calling in favors from all the other agencies around. We even got guys coming down from New York and Chicago to work this thing. But it's a zoo and you should be glad you're in France and not anywhere near Florida right now. You'd quit or go crazy for sure. The whole bunch of them are disgusting. But you know the score. What's the mystery?"

"I need some help with tracking down some information and you are my best guy. But this is going to take someone in Japan. You know anyone?"

There was silence on the far end of the line and I waited a few seconds before asking if he was still there. As I was about to speak he said, "Yeah. I do. But he isn't cheap and he isn't really in my pocket. But he's very good. Is this something really hinky? Or can you find a lot out by just going on Google?"

"I haven't got a clue, that's why I'm calling you."

"Okay, let me sit down so I can take some notes. Go ahead, tell me what you want and I'll decide where I need to dig."

I spent 25 minutes telling him everything about the theft of the kakemono, Yamada, Kenichi Mizushima, the company that did the estate sale, and the buyer of the swords. I tried to give him what background there was on Mizushima, but he interrupted me with several questions and by the time that I finished he summed it up far better than I ever could.

"So you got squat on the thief, right?"

"Pretty much."

"And in order for you to figure out why the old guy kept what everyone thought was a worthless wall hanger when nothing else in the collection was worthless, you want me to find someone who knew Yamada, or who was familiar with the Yamada clan and their fortunes and try to figure out the what and the why. Is that all?"

All? "Um, yeah, Opie, that's all."

"Okay, let me call my guy. I think it's going to take someone in the mix to shake all that out and he's right there in the mix. He did an investigation of a couple businessmen; you know, those Yakuza types, that were shaking down one of the Emperor's personal servants. It got messy, but the Royals were pretty pleased by the way it all got swept under the carpet, or whatever goes for carpeting in Japan. Nothing was ever made public and I think the guy's got some juice where it counts. I'll call him and give him the run down. Let's see what he can find out for us."

"Opie, that sounds perfect. How are Nico and Grindle doing without me?"

"Well, you may have a tough time getting them back. Just warning you, you know... Ellen loves them and my guess is that if she can't pry them away from you, then I'll probably find a couple puppies running around here and biting my toes not long after you come back."

I laughed. "I really appreciate your keeping them for me. I really wanted them to be with a friend."

"No problem. Anything else? I hear sounds coming from behind my door here and I might need to drop the call and jump. Or it might just be more hookers. These people... disgusting..."

"No that's okay. Call me when you have something."

"Will do, Sensei."

He broke the connection and I put the phone on the table to charge.

I took a shower and changed clothes. Suddenly, I realized I had a day free. I had literally nothing to do. I thought about calling Annie and asking her to come out and play, but then realized I really needed to talk to Kara and mend that fence.

She answered on the third ring and didn't seem angry at me anymore. She said she would pick me up and we could go to the old quarter for lunch.

When she showed up I suggested we walk. We started out and had gone only a block when Kara turned and stared at a man on the opposite side of the street. I followed her stare and saw a tall blond man suddenly duck into a small restaurant.

"What is it?"

"I... I thought that was Jean Claude... It looked just like him. But he is somewhere with his sales team... you know? He is doing business, yes?"

"Could it have been him?"

"No." She shook her head. "I have not seen him for three weeks now. It is like seeing him behind bushes?" She smiled ironically up at me.

"You miss him."

"Oh, you know..."

We walked on, but after a few steps she turned back and stared at the door of the restaurant. I could tell she wanted to go back, but felt it would be silly of her to do so. She turned back and then we walked to the tourist center.

It was only a couple miles to the heart of the old city and I liked being immersed in the ancient narrow streets and dim alleys that are tangled like a spider web. The way is cobbled and restaurants and tourist shops line the streets. We walked past several interesting places and finally stopped outside a small boutique. I looked at her for an explanation. She held up a finger.

"*Ah, Kara! Comment ça va?*"

"*Oui, ça va,*" she said.

The man was small and dressed all in black except for the traditional white apron wrapped around his trim middle. He kissed Kara on both cheeks and she did likewise. After chattering rapidly in French for a few moments Kara turned to me and introduced me. I nodded at his lengthy outburst, but did not have a clue what he said.

He turned and Kara motioned for me to follow. We walked through the boutique, down a flight of stairs, across an alley, and then moved perilously down a long, low, dark corridor. When we emerged into a large chamber another man stood waiting and he, too, kissed Kara. We were shown to a table in what appeared to be a dungeon from the Middle Ages, but no dungeon ever smelled like this.

Garlic, fresh bread, seafood, lemon, and herbs of every description, the aromas were overpowering and I felt my mouth begin to water. A waiter appeared with a pitcher and two glasses and he poured the pink wine of the region into them. Another waiter appeared and he placed a tray of raw vegetables and olives on the table along with a crusty loaf of bread.

"Did you order?" I asked her.

"No. They bring you food, here. They decide what you are having. It is like going to a friend's house for lunch, you see… there is no menu; you just eat what your friend brings to the table."

"How do they know what I want? Maybe I'm a vegetarian, maybe I'm lactose intolerant." I was uneasy about the whole arrangement.

"They look at you and see. No one has ever had shoulders like yours who was a vegetarian. And you are in France. Why would you be here if you could not eat cheese? Never. Just wait; you will be happy and if you are not I will take you to McDonalds for a Royal."

"That's just rude."

She shrugged. I realized that despite her nonchalance, she was still irritated with me. I should have known. She never gives up easy.

"Please hand me the bread," I said.

She broke off a piece and handed me the small loaf. I did the same and tried it. It was wonderful. "The olives are from Provence, I presume?"

"Yes," she giggled. She was having fun.

I gave up and sat back and enjoyed an excellent meal. It was themed in seafood, but there were several small dishes that were certainly meat... pork or duck sausage. And the scallops were served on a bed of bitter greens and smothered in bacon. She was right; I loved every single thing they put in front of me and even a couple bites that Kara offered me from her plate. She had been served an entirely different lunch. It seemed to go on forever and when I looked at my watch I saw it was after two in the afternoon and we didn't seem to be anywhere near done yet.

"Do you want to hear what I have found?"

"Yes."

As if on cue we were offered salad and cheese and then coffee appeared. Waiters cleared the table and left us alone then and I told her everything, leaving out only the visits to see Annie. When I was done she sat quietly in thought.

"Do you think that the kakemono was valuable, then?"

"I have no idea, but we need to wait for my friend to see what he can find out. It doesn't make any sense otherwise. Who would want to steal your dojo's Aikido kanji?"

She shrugged. "Speaking of Aikido, the first class of the seminar begins Saturday morning at ten o'clock. Should I pick you up?"

"Don't bother coming over; if Philippe can't pick me up I can get the 81 bus. It only takes about twenty minutes. I don't mind."

She nodded. "What would you like to do this afternoon? Would you like to walk along the beach on our way back?

There should be many half-naked women lying there for you to look at."

This is why it would never work between us. She became jealous and we weren't even a couple. She was angry if I as much as looked at another woman even though she was involved with another man and not in any way bound to me. When we were actually a couple it had been a hundred times worse.

"No," I said neutrally. "Actually I'd like to visit a knife shop. I like to get something interesting when I visit a foreign country."

"France is not a 'foreign' country. You make it sound like you are in Africa…"

"Do you know a place or not; I'm really tired of fighting with you."

She looked up surprised. "We are not fighting."

"Yeah, Kara, we are."

Her face grew pink and she stood up and walked out of the room. I stood and a waiter was suddenly there handing me a check. I reached into my pocket, took out the money and handed it to him and then followed Kara. She had gotten even with me in the best way she knew how, right in the wallet. Still, it had been a lunch I would always remember.

I followed her and we walked eight or ten blocks to a store in the main business district. There were hundreds of knives in the window and I saw something I'd never seen before. It was a folding knife, but the cutting edge was straight as an arrow. It was perhaps four inches long and the handle was made of bubinga, an exotic South American wood that holds a deep sheen from naturally occurring oils. Best of all it was only twenty euros. I would have paid a hundred for it, I liked it that much. So lunch was a wash. I didn't let on. We walked back to Jean Claude's apartment where she'd left her car.

Kara left without coming in and I spent the rest of the day wandering the old city streets just window shopping. Jean Claude's bed looked inviting even before the sun was down, but I forced myself to stay awake reading until it was fully dark. Even that was an effort.

Chapter 18

When I woke up Friday morning I found I was actually excited by the prospects of the day. It would be a long one so I decided I needed a good American breakfast. The market was pulling back the metal gates that protected the glass doors as I approached. I picked up a half dozen eggs, ham, a green pepper, and then went to the freezer section for a small bag of french fries. The bakery across the street sold me a hot baguette and two chocolate croissants.

The streets were quiet, still wet from the street sweepers that come through every morning. I could see the deep blue slate color of the Mediterranean Sea a few blocks away and smell the early morning symphony of humanity on the rise. There was the slightest hint of wood smoke in the chilly air and I realized that October was slipping away.

Philippe was waiting for me outside the vestibule door.

"Sensei, good morning."

"Hi Professor. What brings you around?"

"I like to get up early." He looked at the water and then lifted his nose to the breeze. He smiled.

"You know, Sensei, there have been people coming here to visit and to live from time out of mind. They say the Fertile Crescent is the cradle of civilization and that Africa is the birthplace of humanity, but for me I believe in the matter of choice. And people have chosen the Côte d'Azur for over a half million years. It amazes me to walk down these streets in the early morning like this... to see the old women with their shopping bags and the men sweeping the stairs in front of their place of business. I close my eyes a little and see Roman soldiers bivouacked outside a tent squatting over an open fire. I see early men, not quite human as we recognize such things, doing the same on the cold morning. They are there fanning flames to life while the tribe or the clan huddles together for warmth on the chilly morning. I see people waking to a warm cup of coffee, hands wrapped around the heavy mug to warm them from the chill after leaving their beds." He looked at me in embarrassment.

"This is an ancient place," I said.

"Far more than most realize. That Homo erectus camped right over there," he pointed up the quiet street. "And that Cro-Magnon walked right across this plaza 35,000 years before it was paved... Oh yes, it is a place far more ancient than most ever dream. The Blue Coast has ever been a magnet for those early humans."

"And for us later humans as well," I pointed to the magnificent yachts in the harbor. What brings you here?" I repeated.

"I thought you might like a ride to the university to see what you are made of. This is an American expression, yes?" He laughed.

"Yes, I guess it is, but rarely is it used so literally. I'm going to go up and cook a big American breakfast. Would you like to join me?"

"It sounds dreadful."

"Suffer," I said.

We went in and walked up the stairs to the third floor. I unlocked the door and took everything into the kitchen and then sliced and diced an onion and the green pepper. I then put them on the stove to sauté. The ham went into the small toaster oven, eggs in a skillet, and the french fries I chopped into tiny bits and added to the onion and pepper mix. I'd put coffee on before I left, so I poured us each a big mug and put cream and sugar on the table.

Philippe sat looking distressed during the whole preparation and stared at the plate full of food when I put it in front of him. "It looks awful."

"Just try it."

He took the tiniest bite of egg and looked out the window. A few moments later he took another bite of ham and then tried the potatoes. Eventually he sipped at the coffee and I surreptitiously watched as the momentum of his eating picked up. When we were both finished – his plate was completely clean – I asked him how it was.

"Awful. Really, it was dreadful… really bad. Is there any more?"

I gave him the rest of the potatoes and took a chocolate croissant from the waxed bag.

We sipped coffee.

"Your DNA profile came in yesterday afternoon."

"Did you read it?"

"No. I will explain everything to you at the University. We have a large map of the world and we can follow the path of your ancestors as they came out of Africa and entered the new world. I will try to explain the variations and what all the markers mean. I assume you do not want a course in evolution, DNA, genomics, or natural selection?"

"You assume correctly. I just want to see where I come from."

He nodded. "Whenever you are ready."

I got up and gathered the dishes and washed them. I did not know when Jean Claude was going to return to his apartment, but I wanted it to be clean when he did. I gathered my briefcase and we left.

Traffic was picking up by the time Philippe parked in his assigned place. We walked to the building and into his lab area. Young people were already there at work on computers. At the far end a small group of men were staring at a pile of bones on a steel table. One wore latex gloves and was holding a bit of bone in the air. It looked to me like the others were arguing about it.

Philippe led me into his office and pointed to a chair before a large table. On the wall behind it there was a map of the world. He went behind his desk and returned with another chair. On the table in front of me there was a manila envelope.

"Okay, Sensei. Before we begin, do you have any questions?"

"No."

He opened the envelope and took out a number of pages with charts and diagrams.

"There are over 150,000 DNA markers examined when they do this, it is really quite remarkable."

I nodded. "What's a marker?"

"Each of us carries DNA that is a combination of genes passed from both our mother and father, giving us traits that range from eye color and height to strength or even lactose intolerance. As part of this process, the Y-chromosome is passed directly from father to son, unchanged, from generation to generation down a purely male line. Mitochondrial DNA, is passed from mothers to their children, but only their daughters pass it on to the next generation. It traces a maternal line.

"The DNA is passed on unchanged, unless a mutation, a random, natural, usually harmless, change occurs. The mutation, known as a marker, acts as a signpost. It can be mapped through generations because it will be passed down for thousands of years.

"And it happens all by itself? What if the person doesn't have any children that carry it? Will their children have it?

He smiled at me and shook his head. I should have known better than to ask a question. I felt like a white belt asking the Aiki Doshu a question about Aikido. Idiot.

"When geneticists identify such a marker, they try to figure out when it first occurred, and in which geographic region of the world. Each marker is essentially the beginning of a new lineage on the family tree of the human race. You understand?"

This time I only nodded.

"Tracking the lineages provides a picture of how small tribes of modern humans in Africa tens of thousands of years ago diversified and spread to populate the world. Sensei, by looking at the markers you carry, we can trace your lineage, ancestor by ancestor, to reveal the path they traveled as they moved out of Africa. This is perhaps the greatest advancement in science that humanity has ever taken. Are you ready?"

"Let's go."

We spent the next two hours looking at the charts and diagrams and then up at the map of the world. He told me that there actually is an 'Eve' and we are all descended from only one woman and that she lived 180,000 years ago. She wasn't the only woman around, but is the only one whose line of descent has survived. She gave rise to two different lineages and my own ancestor was from L3 which is the oldest branch to have left Africa. I could have figured that. I have always suffered from wanderlust.

We discussed the passage from Africa and that my paternal line of descent was different. Eventually we moved into a more recent era and Philippe looked up at me with clear happiness on his face.

"Sensei, you have the R0 marker!"

"Okay," I said. "So?"

"This is the lineage of Homo sapien that occupied Western Eurasia around 35,000 years ago, all the way to the Iberian Peninsula."

"Again, okay…"

"You could be a descendant of the man who painted my cave!"

"Yeah?"

"Yes. These were the Cro-Magnon, the early human settlers in France. You are French! Well, partly anyway… there is a lot of Italian, German, and even some Arab, it appears. This is wonderful. Think about it. To be associated with those ancient artists… they were explorers and traveled across vast distances during very difficult times and yet they left us a legacy of magnificent art and obvious culture." He smiled warmly at me and reached out and shook my shoulder.

"What about my American Indian side?"

"Excuse me?"

"My grandfather on my mother's side was Arapaho."

He frowned and looked back at the charts. He picked up the one stack referencing maternal lineage and then the other. Finally he looked at me and shook his head.

"I'm sorry, Sensei. You have nothing in your genome to indicate that any of your ancestors came from the Americas."

"Well, that's not possible. My father spoke Arapaho and we lived next to an Arapaho family. They included us as family, or at least as part of the tribe. They were family."

"I'm very sorry, Sensei, but you were not related."

"Can there be a mistake?"

"No. I'm really sorry, but there is no mistake. It is why we do two different swabs from both cheeks. We actually analyze both and then compare them for consistency. Wait." He looked to the back page and studied the writing there. "No. Again, there is no mistake. You have no American markers at all."

If my Dad was alive he'd certainly have something to say about that. It could only mean that my great-grandmother had been unfaithful. I said as much to Philippe.

"The sad thing about DNA is that it has shown that as many as five percent of births are made by women who have been unfaithful. It is shocking, but there is a strong indication that it is even a survival aspect of the human race. I can give you a book to look at that discusses it. Oddly the Jews have the highest percentage of fidelity of all peoples, but understanding their mating rituals could explain it. You see…"

"That's fine. I'll learn about Jewish mating rituals another time."

"It is in the Koran…"

"I don't care!"

"Sensei, I'm sorry if this has upset you."

"I'm not upset. Well, maybe I am. It doesn't matter. What else does the damn test show?"

We talked for another half hour and I found out that instead of having genetic markers for American Indians I have strong indicators of having descendants on my mother's side from Ireland and the U152 marker from my father's side showed strong indications that he was descended from central Europe. Philippe commented dryly that most Jews come from the same U152. I mentioned that it didn't seem to have caught with my great-grandmother. He didn't have anything to say to that.

"Oh, here is something…"

"What now?"

"Well, it seems that you share about two percent of your DNA with, um, Neanderthals."

"I can't think of a single person who will be surprised. Most especially the women I know."

He smiled at this.

"You do realize that of all the peoples on the planet the populations that mixed with Neanderthals were the most successful as far as developing science, agriculture, higher mathematics, engineering, well, all sophisticated culture…"

"I don't know anything about it."

"It is not politically correct to point it out."

"What?" I was beginning to wish I hadn't asked for the test.

"There are two races of men who did not mix with Neanderthal. There are three that did."

"I thought there was only three races," I said. "Negroid, Caucasoid and Mongoloid."

He waved his hand dismissively. "Old hat," he said. "We now know there are five races. They are based on the continent where they developed. We also know that physical characteristics have little to do with it. For instance there are a number of black Africans and Indians who belong to the race that is associated with Western Eurasia. Skin color and such things have little to do with it. It depends on where your ancestors came from."

"So who didn't get to interbreed with the Neanderthals?"

"The race from Sub-Saharan Africa, those referred to as Africans, and the race associated with the aboriginal people from Australia, New Guinea, and Micronesia, known as Pacific Islanders. The other three races, Caucasians – who consist of North Africans, Western Eurasians and those who come from the Indian sub-continent, Native Americans – both North and South - and Asians, all mixed with Neanderthals and you can see they all developed advanced civilizations."

"I can see why nobody wants to talk about it. It won't make the political correctness hit parade," I said.

He shrugged. "The scientific community knows and don't care. What possible difference could it make to anyone today?"

It didn't matter to me. I was still mad at my great-grandmother.

Chapter 19

"So now would you like to see the galleys of my new book?"

"Yes, as long as we don't have to talk about DNA anymore."

He laughed and led me down a long corridor to another work room that was much smaller than the first. There was a long counter and above it were three very large flat screen televisions that they were using as computer monitors.

"Sensei this is my colleague, Bernard Nocquet."

I offered my hand and he took it. "My pleasure," he said.

"Bernard has been developing the software and the system for developing the photographs we are using in my book."

"How's it going?" I asked.

He shrugged. "It is finished." He looked up at Philippe and added, "Or it will be if they can stop arguing about money and details. My work is done."

"Would you like to see it?"

I nodded and Philippe immediately turned and beckoned me into another small room. There, brilliantly lit on a large table, were stacks of photographs and pages of text. I picked up a large photo and stood struck dumb with amazement.

"What do you think?" Philippe asked.

I did not have an answer. "It's the most remarkable photograph I have ever seen," I said.

He smiled broadly and flipped through the stack. "Here look at this one."

I took it and again had not a word to say. They were photographs, certainly, but it was far more like holding a piece of crystal clear glass and looking through it at something sitting right there in front of me. The image was as real as if the thing were there instead of a piece of paper. I felt as I could reach through it and touch the painted rock wall.

"How?" I asked.

"Bernard? Would you care to explain to my friend how you accomplished this miracle?"

Bernard stepped into the room and leaned with his back to the wall. "We began by assuming that there was degradation of the subject's colors and fine detail. I used the best…"

"I used," Philippe interrupted.

"Yes, of course, Professor." He turned back to me. "Philippe got his hands on the very finest glass lens he could get and took huge digital pictures of the cave paintings under the most intense light he dared. The resulting images were good, very good, but we had a difficult time enhancing them to the degree we felt was optimal."

"When was this?" I asked.

"About seven years ago." Bernard looked to Philippe for confirmation. Philippe waved his hand back and forth meaning close enough.

"So I tried to enhance the images using the normal programs, Photoshop, and what have you, but was unhappy with the results. I wrote a program myself that I felt would do a better, more complete job, but the computer processor was so slow that it took days to do even simple things with the images. Eventually Philippe convinced the University to lease a computer with enough... firepower? Enough speed, Yes? Enough power to move things along more quickly."

"Why did it take so much computing power?"

"The program is not for the photograph," he said. "It is for each and every individual pixel."

I glanced at Philippe and he nodded his head.

"We analyze each and every pixel for color, density, black and white tones, crispness, you see... every characteristic we could imagine. Then we compare them to all the other pixels in the photograph with special attention to the pixels in closest proximity. They are all enhanced, one by one achieving a balance, clarity and color density that you can see is unlike any photograph in the world. And each photograph contains millions and millions of pixels."

"Well, it certainly works. Are you going to be able to reproduce this quality on a mass scale for your book?"

This brought a grim shake of the head from Bernard and a scowl from Philippe.

"Bernard, we will. I told you to have faith. What good is it if the galleys are magnificent and the book is pedestrian?"

"But the cost..."

"We will find the money." He turned to me and continued. "The cost of producing a single photograph like this is astronomical and will make the book too costly for production. We have been experimenting with ways to either bring the cost down or to raise money for subsidizing a first run of books. I believe that once people see the finished product, the book, they will be willing to pay for it. Certainly museums and university libraries... the very wealthy, they should be able to absorb the cost."

"It would be a shame if this was not done," I said. "Is there a timetable for the book's release?"

"The book will be released when I reveal the location of the cave and present the deed to the people of France."

Bernard rolled his eyes. Philippe did not see him.

"You know, I'd think that there are a lot of people, governments, and universities that would be interested in your photo enhancement program. Selling that could generate millions of dollars to…"

"Euros," Philippe said. He could be kind of irritating at times, I saw.

"Fine, euros, whatever, it could generate a lot of money. I can think of lots of applications. NASA could use it to analyze pictures taken from the Hubble space telescope. Militaries would certainly want it to enhance pictures of terrain. Explorers searching for old artifacts in jungles could use it… the list is endless. Searching out poppy fields or marijuana plantations…"

"Yes, yes, we know all this." Bernard stood and looked at me. "But the Professor made an arrangement behind my back with the University. In order to convince them to lease the super computer he arranged that any discoveries, software programs that is, that we wrote would belong to the university. And they have been most interested in this one. They have, in fact, turned the code over to a team of engineers to make it even better and then find a team that will market it commercially."

"Really?" I couldn't help myself.

"Oh yes," Philippe said tiredly. "Can you imagine the man who developed the formula for Gatorade? For the University of Florida? He would be rich beyond the dreams of avarice, but the formula belongs to the University and it is they who are now one of the richest institutions in the world."

"Yeah, living in Florida, everyone knows about that. But wouldn't the university here give you a grant to publish your book?"

"They would and will, but Philippe wants the profit for himself." Bernard said, and then left the room.

"I have poured everything into this project. From developing the cave to this." He waved at the pictures spread on the light table. "I have ignored my family and denied them so much... I need to make something from this to make it right with them and to feel like I have actually accomplished something.

"The cave will bear your name," I said.

"You cannot eat a name. You cannot buy your wife a necklace with a name. You can't give you daughter an IPod with a name." He smiled at me ruefully.

I looked at the pictures there and said, "Why not market the photographs individually? Frame them. Maybe make larger images and frame them and generate profit from that? There are certainly enough photographers out there that sell their pictures to show that there is a market for framed photographs and no one has ever seen anything like these before. People would be looking behind them if they were hung on a wall...""

"I had not thought of that..." he snapped his head around. "Bernard, come in here, please."

He told Bernard my idea, and after an initial disinterest, a purely French disinterest, I could see him warming to the idea."

I said, "You could start with a set of maybe six prints, arrange to sell them through a big gallery, any would be thrilled to have pictures like these... and once the money begins to roll in you could release a snippet to the press suggesting that the photographs were the first wave of a sensational discovery. You know, build interest in the general populace, not just the academic community."

"But how…"

"Just print one twice as large as these and get someone in the art department to mat and frame it. Take it to the most exclusive gallery in Monaco and see what they say. I'll bet you will be shocked at how fast they agree to sell them, and for how much. Then you could take the money and subsidize the printing of the books. Maybe by then the team working on the new technology will find a breakthrough that will bring down the cost."

"But would the University agree?"

"Whose photographs are they?"

"Mine," he said too quickly.

"And mine," said Bernard.

Philippe nodded.

"But not the University's?"

"No," they both said.

Philippe looked at Bernard and Bernard nodded his head and said that if Philippe chose the group he would have them printed and framed. Philippe said he would find a gallery. They forgot I was there.

And whose idea it was.

"Just answer me one last question, Philippe, and I'll find my way out," I said.

"What?"

"Why does it cost so much to make them? The computer time is already subsidized."

"It is the printing. The paper is special, of course, and the printer is from the European Aeronautic Defense and Space Company. It requires special ink that can be atomized almost to the micron level and then fired with exquisite accuracy. It does this while blending colors together to achieve tones and shading unimagined before. It even uses micro texturing to give a sense of dimension and depth. No other printer in the world can do this. We lease the machine and print during off hours at their lowest rates, but even then we have to pay for two engineers to run the machine and of course we both need to be there to make certain that each shot is perfect. It makes the whole process dreadfully expensive."

I was beginning to get it.

"Well, thank you for everything you've shown me, today. At least now when someone calls me a Neanderthal I won't be offended."

He laughed and nodded. "Are you planning to leave? I thought we might have lunch."

"I have other plans for lunch, sorry, but I will see you tomorrow at the seminar, won't I?"

"Of course," he said. "Would you like me to pick you up? I go right past either way."

"Yes, that would very nice. Thank you."

"About 9:30 then, *oui*?"

"Perfect."

Chapter 20

I told the cab driver the address and sat back watching Nice roll by the window. When the driver turned onto the street where Anastasia Poullard lived at her Grandfather's villa, I saw that four men were standing at her gate. I got out, paid the driver and then walked up to the locked iron bars. The men all wore suits, but they could not cover up the hint of tattoos on the wrists and necklines of their dress shirts.

They were Japanese and reeked of yakuza.

"*Pardonnez mai*," I said. I stepped in front of the man standing closest to the gate and rang the buzzer.

I heard Annie say, "*Fiche-moi le paix!* "

"Annie, It's Parker…"

"Parker? Are those men still there?"

I turned and stared at the men. They looked back at me.

"Yes. Is there a problem?"

"I am calling the police."

"Okay, don't ring me in until I call you back."

"Be careful."

I put my back to the gate and crossed my arms. I stood at least a foot taller than the biggest man and easily outweighed them each by seventy or eighty pounds. They didn't seem to be impressed by my display, though, so I let my hands hang at my sides. It is my preferred fighting stance.

The man who appeared to be the leader said something to me in French, but I did not respond. He said something else and again I merely stood looking at him. He turned his head and spoke to the other three men and they all laughed. Then he slipped forward faster than a snake and reached for my throat with one hand, and balling his other into a fist, threw it at my gut.

I guess the sixteen hours I'd spent the previous weekend defending myself against some of Europe's best ukes had left me sharp, because it felt like he was moving in slow motion. I brought my right hand up and deflected his grab with the back of my hand while turning sideways in a half tenkan. As he slipped past me with the power of his missed punch I shoved his head into the iron bars of the gate and he careened off of them and fell to the ground. His knees came up and both hands went to his head.

Blood was washing onto the sidewalk and suddenly the other three men were a whirlwind I could not stop. They had me against the bars and one had taken out a knife when the sounds of approaching sirens stopped them. The man with the knife glanced over his shoulder at the approaching sound and I shoved forward hard and slammed my elbow into his face and then snatched the other two and used my advantage in size and weight to first shove forward and then when they began to turn to me drop back viciously, Their heads and chest slammed together and then both went down cursing. I stepped into the street for more room and then the French police came sliding around the corner and the men grabbed each other up and took off running down the street past the speeding police car.

The police did not have enough room to turn around so they had to back up and by the time they had executed a three point turn I'd heard the sound of a car start and wheels squeal on pavement. The police followed the sounds and I found myself all alone.

I heard a door slam and then heard Annie's voice calling me from the gate.

"Are they gone?"

"Yes."

"I saw them fighting with you. Are you hurt?"

She came out into the street and then led me back to the house. Adrenalin, our old friend, had finally kicked in and I was feeling shaky and slightly nauseous. She led me to the couch, and after I sat went into the kitchen and returned with a glass of red wine.

"You were very brave. But I don't think they would have broken in. Why did they attack you?"

"I don't know other than I was clearly in their way and I didn't show any respect. Or fear," I added.

"You did not look afraid."

"It happened too fast for me to feel much of anything. But fear is a very important emotion. You don't live very long unless you feel afraid once in a while. Fear is our early warning defense system. It generates adrenalin and that makes us very strong and very fast. In Aikido we learn to control adrenalin... let a little out and learn to use it."

"Aikido?"

"Didn't I mention that's what I'm doing here in France? I'm teaching a couple of seminars in Villefranche Sur Mer."

"Oh." She seemed mildly shocked. "You are a *maître de l'aïkido* ? "

I shrugged. "I guess."

She did that pouty thing that French women are all capable of doing when they want to make you wonder what they're thinking, but I didn't bite. I was still trying to wear off the sickness I felt. The knife had done it, I was sure. It isn't every day we face a real blade, and especially one that is wielded by a man you know will kill you.

"Who were they?" I asked.

"They said they knew my grandfather and wanted to come in and talk to me."

"Do you think they knew your grandfather?"

"I don't know. He lived here for a long time. I never saw anyone other than French people visit. My grandmother had many friends and my parents knew many of them, I'm sure, but no Japanese. I never heard him speak it. He never offered to teach either Ken or me… I just don't know if they could have known him or not. But clearly they knew of him. They wanted to come in and in fact they insisted on it."

"Will the police be back?"

"I'm sure of it. I'm surprised they haven't sent another car by now. It is very serious to run from the police and they saw a fight in progress. You will have to answer a lot of questions and they will want to know who you are and what you were doing here."

I stood up and walked to the door.

"Where are you going?"

"Annie, I don't have time for that today. I just wanted to take you to lunch and hoped you would be free. The rest of my day is going to be busy, so I just wanted to spend some time with you."

She pouted again, and then shrugged. "Well we won't be spending much time together even if the police find you here. You should go if you don't want to talk to them. I will say I knew nothing of who you are and let the men explain it if they catch them." She stood.

I nodded and walked to the door. "Can I see you tomorrow?"

"I think I am leaving Nice. My vacation is over next week and I was going to stay until Friday, but if you think my grandfather was a thief, and if those men come back… I don't think I want to be here. I will return to Paris this evening."

"I wish you'd stay."

Again the pout, then she was gently pushing me out the door.

"I liked being with you," she said. "But you are complicated and are not afraid. Men who are not afraid cannot be controlled. I am a quarter Japanese, but still all French, and French women like to control their men. It is why we are better than American women. It is why all men want us. I am just telling you to be honest… You say you felt fear, but you did not. I watched you and you probably don't even know it, but you were laughing when you threw the men to the ground."

She raised up and kissed me. "Goodbye Parker."

I looked deep into her eyes and saw it was not negotiable.

"And you should not have called my grandfather a thief." Then her eyes turned steely.

I hurried two blocks then turned and took the hiking path down to the old city. I was pretty certain the police would not look for me there and equally certain that the yakuza would have remained in their car. The path wound down through trees I could not identify and over steep trails until it finally ended at a stairway that took me down to the paved streets of old Nice. I saw the port across the road and followed it until I arrived at Jean Claude's apartment. It was warm and I had to wonder what would happen next.

The day wasn't exactly unfolding the way I'd hoped. First my great-grandmother and now this; no, it was not unfolding well at all.

Chapter 21

I ate lunch by myself, a ham sandwich, which was great as long as you like a lot of bread and little *jambon.* The mustard was good, though.

It took longer than I'd remembered to walk back to Jean Claude's apartment from Annie's and when I finally got there I thought I could use a nap before my big night at the casino. I spent the next few hours reading, napping and looking at the internet trying to find out as much as I could about the Casino at Monte Carlo.

When I'd gleaned the salient facts and found that other sites were just repeating what I'd already read, a common enough occurrence on the internet, I folded down the lid and got dressed in a sport shirt, jeans and moccasins. While combing my hair I found a painful lump on the back of my skull and figured it must have come from the randori up on the hill. I'd been shoved into the iron gate pretty hard.

Why? In the aftermath of the battle I'd just been happy to have escaped with my life. If the police had not shown up I would probably have been seriously hurt. Four trained, hardened criminals who have been surprised by someone were not likely to play fair. I definitely surprised them. They could hardly expect someone of my training and skill set to just be walking up to the gate. Knives, and even a gun would have appeared and they would have gotten to me.

Annie telling me she was leaving for Paris tonight had completely blindsided me; I hadn't seen that coming. I thought we had made a connection, but on reflection it had all been pretty much whatever she'd wanted. She certainly controlled me while she had me, but give her credit; I'd wanted to be controlled.

I looked around the apartment and checked that everything was in order. Then, taking nothing else but my telephone and wallet I went downstairs to catch the 81 bus and ride it along the coast all the way to Monaco.

It was a glorious afternoon and the after-work crowd was only just beginning to jam the bus when we got to the train station at the bottom of the long hill leading up to the palace. The temperature had moderated over the week and cool breezes were washing over the sun drenched streets. I felt the briskness of autumn winds and liked it very much.

Monique had told me we would all gather at Martin's villa about 8:00 for cocktails and then take a limo to the Casino. Dinner was scheduled for 10:30 and we could go our own way and play both before and then after. I looked at my watch and realized that the bus trip had taken longer than I thought and then slowly made my way to the clothing store.

Standing in front of the mirror was a nice feeling. The tuxedo fit me better than my own skin and did that thing that tuxedos are all supposed to do; it made me look thin and tall and elegant. I turned from side to side and admired my lithe form for five minutes and decided I was going to wear a tuxedo every day for the rest of my life. I wondered if I could do Aikido wearing one. I'd have to think on it.

"*Monsieur*, it is very handsome, yes?"

I turned to the tailor and nodded. We discussed a small alteration and he agreed and took the jacket away for the seamstress to make the small change. I stood and looked at myself again and couldn't help smiling. Bond, I thought, James Bond.

When it was all said and done I told the clerk I would wear it and to just put my old clothes in a bag. I thought he smiled at that, but it was quick and he was turning away. Out on the street I drew not a single glance sauntering up the hill and occasionally checking out my reflection in the store windows.

Eventually I reached Martin's villa and just as I was reaching for the bell I heard the sound of the latch clicking unlocked. Martin's butler pulled the iron door in and ushered me up the path and into the great room of the house.

"Parker, good of you to come. Welcome." Martin was all graciousness and charm. He took me by the arm and led me into the room and up to a man I vaguely recognized who was talking to a man I recognized very well.

"Parker, this is Morrison Falcon and Cash Roberto, Guys, this is Parker. He's joining us tonight. He did a hell of a job on *Above the Fray* as the Martial Arts Coordinator, a hell of a job. He saved Deep's life, too. Can't thank him enough. Enjoy." He turned and walked back to the door where Thad Deep and his wife Valenzuela were being shown in.

I looked at Morrison. He looked way up at me. I thought he was taller. Then I looked at Cash and understood what it felt like to see the Statue of Liberty for the first time.

"I loved you in *Cab Driver*," I said.

He cracked up and patted me on the shoulder. "Marty said you were a funny guy. Talented too, he said you teach a martial art. Aikido? And that thing with Deep... everyone in Hollywood tells a different story, but I heard you got cut pretty bad?"

I shrugged. "Not so bad, I had a metal tool on my belt and it took the brunt of the cut. My student and partner, Curtis got cut from his shoulder to his belt. We thought he was dead for sure. It was bad."

Morrison leaned in and said, "Did you really kill that guy?"

"I thought it had all been hushed up," I said. I was surprised that anyone, least of all two of the biggest icons in Hollywood would know something like that, or even anything at all about me.

Morrison leaned in. "One thing that is certain, Martin never, never forgets when someone treats him well or does something above and beyond the call of duty. You have a friend for life, there." He pointed with his chin and did that little squint thing he does and suddenly I expected the shiny robot to come from around the corner and ask me if I wanted a light saber or something.

His wife walked up and joined us and I was shocked that she is even thinner in person than she looks on television. I was introduced and then Deep walked up with his wife waiting at the other side of the room to make her grand entrance.

"Sensei, it's good to see you." He gave me about fifty percent of his high wattage smile and I felt my knees loosen ever so slightly.

I shook his hand. If they could bottle that smile the military would use it as a weapon.

"Are you still here teaching?" he asked.

I nodded. "I am, although I'll probably talk more about losing my shirt at the Casino when I get home, I'm still teaching another seminar in Villefranche Sur Mer starting tomorrow."

"Hey, I'd like to come take that! I still remember my moves…" He pretended to take a martial art stance and then did a surprisingly good imitation of a *kote gaishe*.

It was my turn to laugh. "You did that pretty well."

He beamed and then Valenzuela cleared her throat and we all turned as she glided across the room. She was wearing an evening gown that someone famous had made, I was sure. She did look spectacular. She preened and everyone complimented her.

Monique was suddenly at my side and for a moment I couldn't catch my breath. I realized I'd never seen her in anything but the standard work day garb or in nothing at all. She was made up in exquisite haute couture fashion and was, without a doubt, by far, the most beautiful woman I had ever seen in my life. It suddenly seemed possible that she was the most beautiful woman any of us had seen because there was not a sound as the group took her in.

Martin leaned forward and said, "Hey, you should get dolled up more often." Everyone laughed and we spent the next half hour mixing in and out of small groups while the rest of the guests assembled. Cash's wife turned out to be a stunning, tall, black woman. I recognized her vaguely from one of his movies. He kept everyone laughing; it turned out he is wickedly smart and has a comedy timing I didn't even suspect.

Eventually the butler moved among us and gathered cocktail and champagne glasses while Martin herded us to the waiting stretch. It was a tight fit and eventually Monique giggled and sat on my lap. That made it comfortable for everyone but me. I worried about wrinkling my tuxedo.

Chapter 22

We drove for no more than five minutes before the limo stopped in front of the grand staircase leading up to the Casino. Everyone climbed out slowly letting the assembled tourists and party goers ooh and aah the arriving celebrities.

I've done so much personal protection work for big shots that it was all pretty casual for me. I took the position I would have taken if I was on duty and then watched Monique pull back slightly and take my arm.

"Hey beautiful," I said.

She looked me up and down and said, "You're pretty gorgeous yourself, Big Guy." She said it in classic Katherine Hepburn. I laughed. Monique can always make me laugh.

We walked up the marble staircase and into the Casino. Everything is marble and gold leaf and elegant beyond imagining. It's like Versailles, or the Library of Congress, or certain areas of the White House. Big, immensely high ceilings that are bracketed with decorations I could not even describe accented walls of polished stone all running down to the marble floor. The place smelled of money.

Then we were in the casino proper and I was surprised. It was actually quite small with only a half dozen tables well separated. I'm used to the big palaces of Las Vegas that seem to stretch on for acres. This elegant room offered no slot machines or mechanical games of any type. Nor did it offer games like blackjack or Texas Hold 'em. Those are all available at the nearby Paris Casino. This rare instution is an elegant place that maintains the gaming traditions of traditional casinos of the past. I knew that the dining room was off the wall closest to the sea and I was certain we would have a table that overlooked the yacht basin.

"What do you think?" Monique asked me.

"Have you ever been here before?"

"No."

"What do you think?"

"I like it." She looked around. "But I was expecting something bigger."

"I'm sure there are other rooms for the high rollers and private rooms for stars and athletes who don't want to rub shoulders with just anyone."

"What do you want to do?"

"I want to break the bank at Monte Carlo." That brought a huge smile.

"Then let's go do it. Do you know how to play?"

"Oh yes, roulette and I are old friends. There are a couple rules about the play here that I had to read up on and they do have one interesting cultural expectation that I found surprising, but actually kind of nice."

"What's that?"

"No displays of either pleasure or distress."

"Really?" She looked startled. "I was going to be your Dallas Cowboys Cheerleader."

She started to do a pompom routine and I laughed and stopped her. "Seriously, I think that one article I read said that a winner's companion was allowed a demure smile, but that might be pushing it."

"Good grief, I thought I'd at least get to high-five you when you win. If you win..."

"C'mon," I said. "Let's find a place at the roulette table." We walked over to the middle table and stood looking it over.

I looked up at the board that records the numbers that have hit. There seemed to be a pattern of sorts and since any game of chance is exactly that, it was as good as I could hope for. I sat down and Monique stood behind me so she would not be in the way if anyone should want to sit at the chair next to me. I reached into my breast pocket, removed my wallet and handed the croupier five hundred euros and indicated I wanted 20 euro chips.

He counted the money carefully twice and then deposited it into a bank and then issued me 25 chips.

"Big spender," Monique whispered.

"Watch and learn," I said, over my shoulder.

Roulette is a simple game that consists of a wheel and a ball that spins inside it and that eventually falls into one of the 37 or 38 numbered slots. They are numbered 1-36 and there are 2 slots that belong only to the house if you are in America, zero and double zero; if you play in Europe there is only one zero. If one of those land everyone betting at the table loses. The numbers alternate being red or black and they are grouped in rows and in blocks. A player can bet on a single number and if it hits it pays 36:1. That's a great payday, but you have 36:1 odds. You can bet on red or black and that pays 2:1. You can bet on a side row of three and that pays 12:1. There are lots of combinations and bets that can be made.

But like all games of chance there is no memory of anything done before and you have no reason to expect that any number or series of numbers will play. I once watched a man sit and play a single number for five hours and not hit once. I myself once hit a red 9 three times in a row and if I had let the bet ride could have retired. As it was I had a lot of fun that year. Still, all that being said, if you look at the board and see that there has been a run of mostly black numbers you can ride that and see how long it lasts. If most of the numbers have been at one end of the board or the other you can try that. I have my own system. But nothing is guaranteed, it is why it is called gambling.

I watched the croupier spin the wheel and saw it fall 10 black. I took 3 chips and placed one each on the 7, 10 and 13 small rows. This covered every number between 7 and 15 with a 12:1 odds bet. If any of those number hit I would win 10:1 because I'd bet 60 Euros total. I call it bracketing. It is my own system and sometimes it works.

The croupier called to place bets and then waved to stop betting and threw the ball. Monique squeezed my arm and I was afraid if we won she would squeal out loud. It rolled around the spinning table and finally bounced into a slot I could not see from my angle while sitting down.

"Eleven, black," he called.

She squeezed even harder but then said in a perfectly upper class British accent, "Oh, I say, Parker... It appears you've won." I glanced over my shoulder and saw her delicately yawning. She was having a hard time doing it while suppressing a big grin, but she pulled it off. I laughed.

The croupier piled the chips in front of me and I pushed them into a separate pile. I took 3 more chips from my active pile and repeated the bet. 20 Euros each on rows 7,10, and 13. I was now bracketing the 11. It was in the same row as the 10. Again it was 12:1 odds.

He rolled the ball and when it hit he called, "Thirty-four, red."

I'd lost.

I glanced at the man to my left and realized he was playing half a dozen individual numbers and playing 500 euros on each number. That came to 3,000 a roll. I was just sitting here playing with chump change. It was a lot to me, though, and I'm willing to place a side bet that I get more juice from a hundred dollar win than this guy did with an 18,000 euro hit.

"Are you going to quit?" Monique asked.

"No, I'm going to see where the table is going," I said. "Is it shifting to the high numbers or was that an anomaly. I'm going to watch."

I didn't place a bet. The croupier finally spun the wheel and flicked the ball in the opposite direction. After a pause he announced that it had come up 2 - black. I put a chip on rows 1, 4, and 7. Monique squeezed. The croupier spun. I lost.

But it had been close. The 11 - black had hit again.

I bracketed the rows and watched as the wheel turned and the ball rolled into 6 – black. I'd won. Monique squeezed my arm, but softer now. She was getting used to the flow of the game.

A waiter came by and we ordered drinks. I played steadily for the next twenty-five minutes and won two more rolls which pushed my winnings pile to 40 chips. I was down to 4 chips in my active pile and bracketed the current group off the 10 – black.

"What are you going to do with that last chip or do you start playing with this pile?" She indicated the winning pile.

"I never play with my winnings," I said. "Not on the same day, anyway. Here, let's tempt fate." I put the single chip on the 11 – black and dared the gods of gambling to hit the same number three times in an hour.

Monique's breath was coming quickly. It was hot and it was in my ear and she leaned against me unconsciously pushing me forward. The croupier called an end to the bets, spun the wheel and then flicked the ball. We watched and suddenly I knew without a doubt where it would go.

"Eleven black," he called out.

"You won?"

"I did. And the hard way. 36 to 1, and because it was also bracketed, 12 to one for a grand total of…"

"Almost a thousand euros," she said.

Thad Deep leaned over me and grinned. "Do you mind?" he said. I moved back and out of his way.

I heard a murmuring around the table as people recognized him. He put 6000 euros down and leaned back. The croupier spun the wheel. He lost. He laughed and said that everyone was gathering in the dining room. I looked down at all the work I'd done to win about two thousand bucks and shook my head. Chump change.

"Sure let's go," I said.

I nodded to the croupier to cash me out, tipped him, and then took the chips he gave me and put them in my pocket. It sure didn't feel like much, but I'd won, just the same.

We joined the group at the table and had a wonderful meal. It wasn't the food, which was delicious, but the company of Cash and Martin. You never hear about certain sides of famous individuals, but Martin was the consummate host, involving everyone in conversation and solicitously making sure that everyone was enjoying themselves. Cash was curious, brilliant, funny to the point of uncontrolled laughter, sensitive and had the ability to make each person at the table the focus of attention and more importantly get others to join in. He was far more impressive in person than he had ever been on the big screen. The force of his personality assumed control of the entire table and even though it was Martin's party, Cash Roberto was the director of the show.

Martin and he were clearly very close. They could glance at each other, smile briefly in passing, and share thoughts. I realized with a start that Martin had directed several of his movies and then began to understand the movie business a little better.

Eventually Martin said, "Okay, let's see if I can finally win and take some money off that damned Arab."

Everybody laughed and took their time getting to their feet. We followed a waiter as he led us out a side door and into a long corridor.

"Where are we going?" I asked.

"Each year Marin plays baccarat with some old friends and they have a private room here in the Casino. He usually loses." Monique squeezed my hand.

We followed them all into a small room with a raised table surrounded by plush chairs. Morrison, Deep, Scarlotti, and Roberto all took chairs at the table.

"C'mon Parker, we got a chair for you, too."

"Sorry, Martin, I don't know the first thing about baccarat and I don't gamble my money at things I don't know about. I wouldn't even gamble your money at this." I waved vaguely at the table.

"Suit yourself," he said. "But enjoy the champagne and buffet." Then he turned to the table and seemed to grow serious. There were half a dozen men already at the table and they all wore grim expressions. No one joked. Morrison's wife slipped over and said, "He's never played before," indicating her husband. "He's nervous."

He should have been. Over the next hour he lost over 25,000 euros. The play flowed from one player to the next and when I thought I'd finally figured out the play someone would win and suddenly people were taking percentages of the stakes and forming and reforming partnerships and I had not a clue what was happening. Clearly the audience was not expected to comment and so I couldn't even ask for explanation from anyone. Monique came back to my side and whispered, "What do you think?"

"I think Martin is winning slightly, Morrison is losing badly, and the others are holding their own."

"That's not what I meant."

I looked at her.

"Do you want to stay and watch?"

I shrugged. It was Martin's party. On the other hand, she looked devastating in her dress...

"What do you want to do?" I asked.

"I want to watch you play roulette."

"I told you I never gamble with my winnings."

"You said on the same day," she smiled. She reached out and took my hand and lifted it up so she could point at my wrist. "It's tomorrow."

Chapter 23

We walked to the main floor and looked at the tables. There were many more people here than before. After a few minutes we saw a large woman rise and leave an empty chair at the center table. We slipped into the vacancy and I took out the Casino's chips from my pocket. There was a little over 1,900 euros. I kept the change and handed the croupier the 1,900 and asked for 100 euro chips. Now I would look like everyone else playing at the table if nothing more.

The board showed a lot of hits in the lower third; some were in the high twenties and many in the thirties. I played the bottom three rows with one hundred each. The croupier called for all bets and then spun the wheel. The ball fell into the slot for back 8. I'd lost. I looked up at the board and saw few in the single digits but then figured the board might be changing so I bracketed the 8 by placing 100 Euro chips on the 4, 7, and 10 rows.

Monique stood very close behind me and I felt her hand on my shoulder. Her breath smelled sweet, with the slightest hint of champagne. When I glanced back at her I saw moisture on her upper lip. She squeezed my shoulder and pointed back at the table with her chin. The wheel spun and the ball rolled and then the croupier was calling black 31. I'd abandoned my strategy and lost again.

I had 13 chips still in my pile and decided the hell with it. I bracketed the 31 row by placing chips on the 28, 31, and

34. I thought about it and decided I was ready to be done playing. I added another chip to each pile. The game didn't feel good anymore. I'd already won and now I was just throwing away my winnings, something I'd long ago sworn never to do.

The croupier called, 36 red, and just like that I was even. He pushed 24 chips over to me and I moved them to my right, into a winning pile. Monique was squirming behind me whispering congratulations. The crowd had grown and I could sense the body heat and the smell of very expensive perfume. I was being pressed into the table and wanted to stand and leave, but decided that one more play would finish it.

"What number did we hit for the jackpot earlier?" I asked.

"Eleven. I can't believe you don't remember."

I looked at the 7 chips still in my play pile and put them all on black eleven.

"You're going for it? Oh, God, Parker, this is so exciting…"

"Just hold on. It's nearly impossible odds to hit on the same number in one evening."

She reached around and gently took my chin and pulled my face around. Her tone was not gentle. "It's tomorrow, damn it!" Then she grinned.

"Place your bets." I turned around and then watched him spin the wheel and flick the ball in the opposite direction. It rolled and the wheel turned and suddenly I realized she was right. More than just right, I knew with a sudden intuition that I was going to win. The wheel slowed and I turned to Monique and waited for her to look at me and then to meet my eyes and then I smiled my biggest, killer grin at the very same time the croupier called, "Eleven Black."

This time, a lot of people forgot the 'no display' admonition, because everyone in the place made some kind of noise. A number of people offered me their congratulations and there were oohs, and ahhs from people in the crowd as the croupier pushed the pile of 252 chips over in front of me to add to the 24 already there. I motioned for him to cash me out and he counted and recounted the pile and then converted it to the house chips. These chips weren't round. I tipped him and then Monique and I slowly sauntered to the cashier.

The counter is in the back of the casino in an alcove that leads to offices. I asked for 500 cash and handed her my American Express card and asked that the rest be credited to my account.

"Yes?" She looked at a man standing behind her and he nodded and shrugged.

"Is that a problem?" I asked.

"No. Actually, although very unusual, it makes a lot of sense. You have nothing to carry and it is now easy to spend." She smiled slightly.

We found a waiter and asked to be taken back to the baccarat game.

They were taking a break. Monique was still very excited about the win and told the group I'd broken the bank. Martin looked at me in shock and I shook my head, no. I held my thumb and forefinger about a half inch apart and everyone laughed.

"I'm ready to go, though. I have to teach tomorrow and it's already very late."

Martin shook my hand, thanked me for coming, and told me I would always be welcome if I ever wanted to return for a visit.

I said good night to the rest of the group and for the first time that I'd known her Valenzuela offered me her cheek to kiss. I was practically shocked. Martin told us to use the limo, that he'd be playing for a couple more hours and would not need it.

"Just send it back," he said.

We left and as we descended the marble staircase I felt like I'd just had one of the more interesting evenings of my life. The limo door was open and James, the driver, was waiting.

I slipped my hand into Monique's and sat shoulder to shoulder with her as we moved slowly up the hills through the dark night.

"Parker, it was really good to see you again." She leaned her head on my shoulder. "I need to tell you something, though. When I first saw you walking down that sidewalk I was feeling really bad about my life. Sure, here we were in Cannes and I was sitting with these famous people and living the high life, but I was so lonely I can't begin to describe it.

"And then there you were. Like the nameless Samurai in a Kurosawa movie you came walking down the sidewalk bigger than life. Everyone was moving out of your way and you were smiling and a head taller than everyone else. My God, you took my breath away. And then I acted like a complete fool."

"You didn't act like a fool, Love, you acted like the woman I wanted to marry. I was overjoyed to see you."

"Hush, don't make things up. Still, there is still a part of me that wants you so badly I can't stand it. I want to be married; I know that now. I want to make some babies and watch them grow and I want to go to bed at night with a man I love and wake up with him in the morning. I want to grow old with him."

I didn't know where this was heading, and kept quiet. I wondered if I still wanted to marry her and what I would say if she suggested it. I imagined it for a second and then decided I did.

"But Parker, we're leaving for Africa tomorrow night and I want that, too. I want to go around the world searching for locations to shoot movies and then to plan and work and stay up all hours in front of a script and then try to talk to actors and get them on board and make a movie. I love making movies and can't imagine not doing it. There is something special and magic and lasting about that kind of effort and I worry that if I give it up and then watch my babies grow and then go off to college and see my husband sitting on the couch and grunting at the things I say… will I just despair for ever having given it all up?"

We were back to square one. This is how it had ended the first time. The door opened and the driver offered Monique his hand to help her out. I started to follow her up to the door where the butler stood waiting, but she turned to me and gave me a fierce hug.

"Goodbye Lover. James will take you back to Nice. Just tell him where you're staying. I… I want you to know that whenever I think about going to bed with a man and getting up in the morning, about giving birth and that man sitting at my side holding my hand.., when I think about birthdays and pony rides for the kids… well, each time I imagine it, the man has your face." She looked up at me and held my eyes with hers. Then she turned and walked through the gate and up to the villa. The butler walked slowly over to the stretch and handed me the shopping bag with my old clothes. He turned and walked back. I got into the limo and told James to take me to the Port in Nice, then I sat back and enjoyed the ride. It's what I do.

Chapter 24

The next morning I was waiting for Philippe at the corner when I saw him weave through traffic and practically slide to the curb. I got in.

"How are you, Sensei? Did you break the bank?"

"I understand a gentleman never discusses such things," I said.

He turned to look at me. "So you did well then."

I shrugged.

"Maybe you would like to pre-order a book?"

It was my turn to look at him. "Maybe."

"Well, well… Do you think that five thousand is too much for a copy?"

"It's pretty steep. I don't think you'll sell many at that price."

"At that price I don't have to sell many."

I thought about it. The cave had been something beautiful and precious and something only a handful of human beings will ever see in person. The book would remind me of it and might even, in a perfect world, retain some of its value. And what was the money for, after all? It was found money. I decided.

"Okay, Professor, I will pre-order a copy of your book on one condition."

He frowned. "And that would be..?"

"That you inscribe it to me, and that you include in the inscription that we visited the cave together and I got to see it firsthand."

He laughed. Then he thought about it. "Yes, I can see how that would make it much more special and valuable to you. Alright. It is a deal. Where is my money?" He held out his hand and we both laughed.

The seminar was crowded and I knew it would be difficult to teach an energetic, physical class with so many people on the mat, so I decided to do something I had wanted to do for ages.

Once the class was bowed in and warmed up I told everyone to sit comfortably and asked Kara to interpret for me. Most of the black belts and about a third of the white belts remained in seiza, the classic Japanese sitting position on their knees. This was meant to impress me with the fact that they were such Samurai in the spirit that this was to be construed as comfortable.

I lifted my hakama and my gi trousers and showed them the scars from all the surgeries I'd had.

"This is from sitting in seiza," I said. "My ancestors evolved in Western Eurasia and did not sit on their knees. I am not built to do this and the result of my doing it was a great deal of damage over the decades. If all of you come from people who evolved in the Asian area, then you might actually be okay with it. It's your choice."

I pointed to a few of the black belts in the front row and then back to my knees as Kara interpreted this. There were many frowns and aloof looks but the majority of the white-belts immediately dropped to sitting with crossed legs. A few of the black belts joined them. I shrugged. In France it's catching.

I spent twenty minutes talking about the idea of Aikido principles. How we center, triangulate, and allow the attack to come and then establish a nexus of energy to lead it to a forward or rear break point. I spoke of strategy and technique and humility. I explained how the uke brings all the energy and how, if the nage is performing correctly, he contributes nothing. I talked about dissolution of energy and not bringing extra force to the purpose of executing technique and how we never use a breakfall unless uke's energy absolutely demands it.

I then had them stand and began to lead them through techniques that were designed to emphasize all of the principles individually.

Noon came and everyone expected me to end the class when I had them sit, but I demonstrated another technique. I talked at length about how the attack changed as uke moved toward nage, how each step and each inch of closure alters nage's perspective and ability to accommodate the attack until he is left with only one choice.

This is the essence of resolution itself. It is why when we are training and are expected to perform a particular technique over and over no matter what the uke does, it is not really Aikido at all. It is, at best, technique training. Aikido is resolution. We have to wait until uke closes and we create the nexus before we can possibly know what the technique will be.

They stood and trained. I let thirty minutes go by and did nothing but watch. People began to watch the clock. I taught several more applications of applied principles. Another hour slipped by.

Kara came over and was clearly upset. "I'm going to end the class. People are hungry and we are supposed to be having a break."

171

I looked at the clock. It was 3:00. The class had been going now for five hours. I turned to her and said very quietly, "No. you are not going to end this. We are finally getting somewhere."

She glared at me. "This is my dojo. I'm ending it."

I looked at her and we locked eyes. It has always been this way with this woman. It has always been a test of wills. I thought about what Annie had said to me and suddenly realized she had been correct. Kara was demanding that I break before her will and that I allow her to control the situation, just like always.

I called Philippe over and asked him to translate for me. I dismissed Kara with a wave of my hand, and then clapped both hands together and called seiza. When they were all seated I looked at Philippe and then made a show of looking at the clock.

"I understand it is now well past your lunch time. I also understand perfectly well that you are now out of your comfort zone." I paused and Philippe translated. "I am teaching you something very rare and very special because I was convinced that the French Aikidoka are rare and special." That brought tired smiles. "I am not done yet, we are not there yet, but I also understand that certain weak individuals, people who really don't want to study Aikido for the ultimate knowledge, but only wish to train in it because it is popular... I can see how those types of people might want to leave. So those of you who are like that, those who wish to leave just when we are reaching the truth... you may go now." I waved my hand toward the door.

No one moved. I gave it a long five count and then turned to Philippe and asked him to attack. We continued to train. Hour after hour we trained until finally, I saw a young man of about thirty suddenly sag. His uke attacked and his response was barely perceptible, but his uke snapped around, his feet glided out from under him and he gently rolled over his head. He attacked again and it seemed the nage was moving in slow motion, almost as if he was under water and the result was the same. They switched roles and the same thing happened. It was master level Aikido. They could each have been Osawa Sensei when he was eighty years old. They were perfect.

I walked up to a couple men and motioned for them to sit and to watch. I did this over and over until the whole dojo was sitting in a huge circle and watching the two attack and resolve. Everyone in the dojo sat and watched mesmerized. There was not a soul in the room who could not see or who did not understand what was happening to these two exhausted people. They had left their bodies behind. Their bodies were performing with a piece of their soul rooted into the very center of the universe. They were outside, looking in and merely watching as the core functions of their brains were united with a spirit and a connection to the Divine that few ever embrace. They were experiencing grace.

It took a couple minutes for them to even be aware that the class had stopped and students were sitting quietly watching them. When they became aware they stopped and sank to their knees.

I softly motioned to the group to line up and when I sat and turned I saw many of the students with tears flowing down their cheeks. Several had their arms closed across their chests and seemed to be completely overwhelmed with emotion.

I turned and quietly bowed and then stood and walked off the mat. They could all bow to each other if they chose but I needed to get off the mat. I had tears flowing as well.

Philippe dropped me off at Jean Claude's apartment. I went upstairs and sat looking at the kitchen stupidly. I didn't realize at first why, but then it occurred to me that I was exhausted. I showered and went to bed with an empty stomach. I was so tired I never heard the telephone ring and so I never spoke with Opie and didn't hear what he had found out for me. All in all, in retrospect, that was a good thing. If forewarned is forearmed, then it would have caused crashes and sirens to sound when what I needed in the end was mere silence.

The next day I simply taught classes and the seminar ended at 1:00. Afterward students came up to me to thank me for the seminar and in particular for the previous day. They all said they felt uplifted, emboldened, and as if they truly were beginning to understand.

I figured that was about as much as any sensei can hope for.

Chapter 25

Kara and I sat in her office and did the money thing. It's the part of seminars most people don't think about, and the part that senseis do it for. Oh, I guess some people are so desperate to be recognized that they will travel and teach for nothing. Hell, some are so desperate for recognition that they will travel at their own expense to teach or demonstrate. I won't. I will certainly do it to help one of my students become established and to raise money for them, but I'm running a business and if I have to work a second job to keep the bills paid, somebody is going to pay me. Especially when you see a hundred people on the mat at a hundred bucks a throw. There is a lot of money being made in these things by someone.

Kara showed me her receipts and calculated my cut and then wrote out a check. I put it in my briefcase. She was still angry at me for dismissing her yesterday, but she was also being careful as she had made a ton of money over the last two weekends.

"So you will be going home now?"

"I'll book a flight tomorrow," I said.

"And you never found my kakemono. That is very sad."

Several students were talking loudly about something outside her office and suddenly she shot up and walked out of the room. There began an intense discussion in French with all three people speaking at the same time. I took my foot and shoved the door closed and then opened my phone to see if I had any mail.

I saw that Opie had called and then looked at my watch. It was 8:30 in Florida. I hit the icon below his picture and he picked up on the third ring.

"I was wondering if I was going to hear from you."

"What did you get?' I stopped. "Hold on, first how are my dogs?"

"They're fine. Stop worrying about them. You should worry about if you'll ever get them back."

"Right, like that's going to happen. Okay, what did you find?"

"Well, it's interesting. Yamada is an old Samurai family with a hell of a history. They had their own castle and kingdom and all that shit before the country was united. You know, like five hundred years ago. Afterward they were favorite retainers of the Emperor, but the family holdings and fortunes pretty much dried up over the centuries except for this one stash of priceless family heirlooms. It turns out that the Yamada treasure was actually kind of famous. It had a number of things that were, or should have been, in the national museums and Emperor's palace."

"Like what?"

"Well, there was this assortment of buttons... I know, weird, right? But the first Shogun – he was kind of like Castro - wore them and they were his favorites, so they were supposed to be priceless. And there were a bunch of swords, naturally, but these were all made by the big shots in the sword making business. They were supposed to worth millions. And there were other things, paintings and suits of armor that some famous guy wore. There was even..."

"What kind of paintings?"

"Hang on, let me get my notes." I listened to two minutes of silence and then he came back on the line. "There was a collection of sumi-e paintings... let me spell that for you..."

"I know how it's spelled. Why are they so special?"

"They're old, and all done by masters. You know like a Japanese Rembrandt or Picasso or something."

"You got any names?"

"Nothing that I've ever heard of. Oh wait. Yes, there was. An author, the guy wrote a book and apparently he was a painter too. His name was Miyamoto..."

"Musashi," I finished. "Probably dated sometime around 1640 or 1645. Right?"

"Don't have any dates, but okay. You know him?"

"For Christ's sake, Opie, every martial artist on the planet knows him. They call him the Sword Saint. He killed like sixty people in individual combat with a sword. He's Japan's most famous warrior. He's like King Arthur only they know he actually existed because he left a long legacy. Are you telling me that one of Musashi's sumi-e paintings was among Yamada's personal family wealth?"

"Yes, Parker, I guess I am. Pretty big news, huh?"

I couldn't believe it. This went way beyond any lost personal tokanoma or swindle involving stolen antiquities. This involved a stolen nation treasure.

"So what happened to the Yamada estate?"

"Hold on." I heard paper rustling. "It disappeared sometime during the occupation. Apparently this Admiral Yamada put it all in storage when he went off to war. Then when he came back he took it out, but before he could do anything with it the allies came by and picked him up. He was in prison for about five years and when he was finally released everything was missing. No one has a clue what happened to any of it. I mean, according to my guy, there was chaos in the streets and former peasants were making fortunes and former rich dudes were begging. The whole culture was on its ear and the allies still held sway for a long time. And they didn't much give a shit who got fucked over because they were all remembering Pearl Harbor. Nobody got much sympathy that their personal fortune had been stolen."

"Yeah," I said. "War does that to countries, especially when you lose in a big way. They ought to be glad it was Americans who won. At least we helped them put it all back together. If Russia had taken over they'd have stripped the country dry and everybody in Japan would be speaking Russian."

"And we wouldn't have Toyotas and a Sony Walkman stuck in our ear."

"Sony is yesterday's news."

"Whatever. Did you get what you need?"

"Yeah, thanks.

"Good, because it was expensive."

"How much?"

He told me and I shivered.

I put my phone away and sat there considering. Was it possible? Was it even remotely possible? Was that smeared, faded piece of rice paper a brushwork by Miyamoto Musashi? Basically lampblack ground exceedingly fine, a brush and a little water, thinned, dipped, applied by special masters who have trained for decades... was Kara's kakemono a five hundred year old masterpiece covered and lost to the world now by someone who just wanted an Aikido kanji, or was it now in the hands of a world class thief who had a precious, irreplaceable masterpiece worth hundreds of millions of dollars...

"Sensei?"

I looked up. Curtis was standing in the doorway. I hadn't even heard him open it.

"Hey Curtis, what's up?"

"Hi Sensei. Are you angry with me?"

"Why would I be angry with you?"

"Well, I was on the mat with you for two days and you never once spoke to me or called me to be uke for you. I just wondered if my going off with that young woman upset you."

"I don't care who you sleep with. I didn't call you because you train with me all the time and I wanted to let the students here have a crack at me. I'm not that shallow that I won't use someone to further Aikido just because of some personal bullshit. I just didn't think you needed any special attention. You were doing fine, as you should have been as one of my chief instructors. Don't worry about it."

"Okay. Thanks. Yesterday was really something."

"It worked." I looked at my phone.

"Sorry, I didn't mean to interrupt."

"Come in and sit down for a second. Do you know what all the screaming is about?"

"I don't know. Every time it dies down someone else starts getting loud. I thought I was beginning to catch a little of the language, but I don't have a clue what's going on. Are you still staying at that apartment?"

"Yeah. I was going to book a flight for tomorrow or Tuesday, but something interesting just came up. Where are you staying? Still hooked up with the hottie?"

"No. We had some control issues. It was her way or she'd pout and act bitchy, so I let her pout one day and the next day she was gone." He shrugged. It was catching.

"I understand all about control issues," I said.

"The sensei, here?"

"Oh, yeah. French women like to have it all, including your…"

"Your what?"

Kara was standing in the doorway now and by the look on her face was furious with someone.

"Kara come in and sit down. We need to talk. Curtis, would you please stay here and listen as well?"

She pouted and then came and sat. She had her arms crossed and her chin practically rested on her chest. I looked at her for a long moment, reflected on our long history and then for the briefest moment thought of Monique and how she could always make me laugh. I suddenly didn't care about Kara and her pointless power games.

"You might have been robbed by a professional and you might have been robbed of something really special," I said. I spent the next twenty minutes laying out the entire investigation and what I had just learned. She slowly sat upright and then she began to look amazed. The amazement soon became fury.

"You have to find it!"

"I will say it again, Kara, I don't speak French and it will be very hard to even discover if that piece of rice paper you covered up was actually a Musashi of not. I can try to find out who bought the paintings from the liquidator, although my welcome there was pretty much used up. I can try to find out if they are now trying to sell a Musashi. If they aren't… well it's also possible that Kenichi Mizushima might have sold it off decades ago to fund whatever he was doing with his life. Of course the same is true of all the other things he was supposed to have. If, of course, he did actually steal and import the entire fortune, and not just a few pieces of it, then it is also possible that the kakemono you bought for a few dollars was one of the sumi-e that were stolen."

"It was so long ago. Who cares?" She pouted.

"Kara, you understand that even if you get it back you can't keep it."

"What?" She burst into a long diatribe in French and I glanced at Curtis. He caught my look and sadly nodded his head.

"You can't keep it, Kara, it's a Japanese national treasure. You would be required to report it and then turn it over. I'm sorry."

I thought she would begin to pout again, but she actually sat up and then brightened. "I could just take it to Japan and then present it to Doshu. That might be worth a promotion, don't you think? Or at least a visit by him to my dojo..." She looked around. "My little, humble dojo..."

She was always a step ahead, always plotting. Actually turning it over to Doshu, the head of all Aikido, the founder's grandson, would be a hell of a shot in the arm for Aikido though, as he could then reasonably expect to be the one to turn it over to the President or the Emperor or some other big shot and get some juice for himself and all of Aikido.

"Whatever. If you want me to keep looking and to find what I can, you are going to have to loan me your car for a few days or rent me one. I'm done with busses and trains and walking. I'm an American and Americans might start out by walking, then start to jog, then they might run, but we always end up right where we belong... driving. Get me a car."

"Fine! Let's go, though. I have things I need to do." She stood and we followed her. I looked at Curtis and then realized we had not finished discussing his current situation.

"Where are you staying? Can we drop you off?"

"Um, I'm going to have to get a hotel room, I think. I was staying with one of the students for the last few days, but he is leaving town and hinted that I had to go."

"Fine, no problem. You can stay with me. There's a futon couch that folds down and is better than a floor somewhere. It's a pretty big apartment. You can help me figure this thing out, too, if you want."

"Great. I was really hoping to see some of the Côte d'Azur. I spent all of last week in Italy."

"We might have to go over to Marseilles to check out a gallery. We could drive along the coast and have a great bottle of wine and some bouillabaisse while we're there. It's supposed to be the specialty of the region."

"I read Ian Fleming years ago when I was kid."

I looked at Curtis and wondered what the hell that meant, but didn't bother asking. He's too well read, too smart, too flat out brilliant for me to completely understand at times. I let it go.

Kara was putting her gi and hakama in the trunk of her car.

"Why didn't you ride with Philippe?" she asked.

"He didn't come today," I said. "He said he needed to spend some time with his family."

"Bof," she uttered. "He always has a family for an excuse."

She climbed in. Curtis and I looked at each other and followed. The next two hours were spent in negotiating traffic and renting a car big enough for me to fit reasonably in. In France that turned out to be a luxury model and Kara was furious that I was unwilling to drive several hundred miles with parts of me sticking out the windows of the sub-compact car that she wanted to rent for me.

"I think we should go back to the apartment, drink a lot of wine and then walk to a nice restaurant."

"I think that's a great idea, Sensei. I'll even buy you dinner."

"I don't need you to buy me dinner, but there is something you could do for me."

"Name it," he said.

I tossed him the keys.

"Drive," I said.

Chapter 26

The next morning we drove over to *Riviera Les Ventes de Liquidation*. I told Curtis to just drop me off and then circle the block. It shouldn't take a minute to find the name of the art dealer who bought the wall hangings.

When I entered the room went oddly quiet. It looked as if the place had been rearranged and things broken in the process. Several machines were on the floor in pieces and a file cabinet had been turned over and all the papers scattered. A young woman came over to me and asked if she could do something for. At least that's what I assumed she said. I pointed to the door of the office of the gentleman who had given us the information the first time we'd been here and he looked up just as I pointed in his direction. He got up slowly and when the young woman approached him he solidly shut the door in her face.

"You should leave." I turned to see a powerful, tall man standing on the other side of the counter.

"I just…"

"Leave, now!" He pointed toward the door.

My childish side was welling up in me, but I held it in check and simply turned and walked out the door. Curtis was cruising down the street and I climbed in.

"Did it go well?" he asked.

"No. We need to find those documents."

Before we had gone to dinner the night before I had taken my briefcase apart looking for the documents on the liquidation sale. I didn't have them. They were not in the apartment and that could only mean that I had left them with Annie. This was a huge mistake on my part.

"Go down this street until we pass the big curve and then take a hard left. We have to see if she might still be there."

He did as I asked and then followed my directions to the villa on top of the hill between Nice and Villefranche Sur Mer. We turned onto her street and then I directed him to stop in front of the gates. I got out and tried to see into the parking area, but it wasn't visible from the gate. The place didn't seem to be occupied, but I tried the intercom anyway. I was just getting ready to turn back when a male voice said, "*Oui?*"

"Hello, I'm looking for Annie Poullard. My name is Parker."

"The Aikido Sensei. Yes. One moment, please."

I was surprised. It had to be her brother. I watched as a small, dark man walked from the door to the gate. He looked me up and down.

"You are Parker, yes? Annie told me about you. She has gone to Paris, I'm sorry."

"And you must be Ken, her brother. She told me about you as well."

We stood and looked at each other. "She told me she enjoyed you very much."

We still just stood and stared at each other.

"I enjoyed her as well," I finally said.

The corner of his mouth twitched. I was speaking about his sister for heaven's sake. Is there no limit to the depth of a man's ability to roll in the gutter with pigs? There may be, but I'm not sure I've ever seen it.

"Then you might as well come in. What can I do for you?"

We walked into the house and he led me to the kitchen.

"I was with your sister here last week and we discussed some documents I had received from the company that did your grandfather's liquidation. I thought I had brought them with me when I left, but apparently I left them here with her. I need to have those documents, or at the very least look at them. Is there any way you can contact her and see if she put them somewhere?"

"Why would the details of my financial life interest you?" His voice was mild, but his eyes looked as piercing as a snake.

"I'm trying to find something that was stolen from a friend of mine."

For the next ten minutes I carefully massaged the details of the story to try and convince him to call Annie or at the very least look for them among her things, all without calling his grandfather a thief.

"You are implying that my grandfather was a thief."

"I didn't say that."

"There can't be any other explanation." He walked across the room and sat in a chair overlooking the pool area.

I walked over to him and said, "Ken, do you know what's going on?"

He rubbed his jaw line and stared at me. "You aren't the only person who is looking."

"I'm not?"

"Yakuza came here yesterday and forced me to show them Grandfather's room. They found nothing. I told them they should go to the liquidator's offices and speak to them.

It is out of my control now. Everything he had is gone, except for the villa and Annie and I are keeping it." He motioned toward another chair and I sat down.

"I believe that you were cheated by the liquidators."

"Maybe so, but if everything that they sold was stolen goods and goods that could be claimed by Japanese officials as national treasures, then what we got was the best we could get. Better than having it confiscated.

"So you knew?"

"I suspected."

"About everything? Did you know the details of the treasure?"

"No, only that it might not belong to my grandfather. It mostly all carried the crest of an old samurai family called Yamada."

I nodded. "Did you tell the liquidators about that?"

He looked at me like I might be crazy. He didn't need to answer any further. I couldn't think of anything else to ask so I returned to my original request. "Can you call Annie and see if she left the papers here?"

"I'll go look." He got up and walked out of the room and was gone most of ten minutes. When he came back he carried a sheaf of papers and I recognized my handwriting on the very top sheet. He sat and slowly looked through them. "What are you specifically looking for?"

"I need the name of the art gallery that bought the wall hangings. What they called framed art."

He shuffled papers and then looked up at me. "The man's name is Francis Poirot." He wrote out the name of the shop and the address on a small piece of paper and handed it over to me. "Which piece is so important?"

I told him about the discount table and Kara finding the split bamboo scroll. She was certain she could use it for the dojo's shrine so she bought it. I mentioned the netsukes as well. At this his eyes lit like a dark fire kindling in coal black caves.

"The netsukes, yes. These I believe were stolen from us by *Riviera Les Ventes de Liquidation*. I believe that they hired the woman to come in and offer to buy all of them for next to nothing. When I found out that none of their special dealers had made an offer for them, and they were just scattered like so many broken toys on a table top... well, I could not believe that they did not know what they were. This we fought about."

"I thought it pretty odd myself; that they could be so cavalier with your belongings..."

"Cavalier? No, they were outright thieves. I hope the Yakuza shake them until they find what they are after."

"What were they after?" I asked.

"I don't know."

"Well, I think that the yakuza already paid them a visit." I told him about the mess I'd seen in the office and of the hostile attitude by the people there.

"*Bon.* I hope they shook them until their eyes rattled in their heads."

I couldn't think of anything else to say to him so I stood and offered my hand.

"I will tell Annie you came by and remembered her."

"Thank you. She's pretty hard to forget."

"She said the same of you."

I left and found Curtis standing at the intersection looking out across the Mediterranean Sea.

"What an amazing view!"

I found that I'd already grown used to it, but smiled just the same.

"Yes, it is."

"Did you get what you wanted?"

"I have an address and soon, with the help of Google Navigator, we are going on a road trip."

"How soon is that?"

I held up my telephone and turned to go back to the rental car. "As soon as you can fire it up and get us off this mountain," I said.

Chapter 27

We drove as slowly as the French drivers would allow, but still made it in just a little more than two hours. The gallery was in the seventh arrondissement, or district, and in the section of old town called Saint Lambert. Rue Crinas wound tightly through narrow buildings and made a hard left turn, almost a u-turn right where the gallery sign thrust out over the sidewalk. Curtis parked in a space I would not have believed possible, the Volvo sedan had no more than two inches to spare on either end.

The address was odd. It indicated that we were at the building, and we could see art works through windows, but there was no door to enter. There was a door, but clearly no business that sold art would allow the public to use it. It was hard, strong and ugly. I thumbed my phone and called up Navigator, then looked at the map again.

The street made a very sharp left turn just ahead and almost doubled back on itself. Actually it did double back for the length of about two blocks then cut back in its original direction.

"C'mon," I said. We walked toward the curve and then followed the sidewalk up a hundred yards and found the entrance. "These businesses must have the entire building, front to back."

Curtis looked at the sign and then said, "Do you want to do it like we planned?"

"Sure. Think of it like a game."

"Okay." He opened the door and walked in. After a moment he opened the door and nodded his head. He stood there with his back to the open door and waited for me to go through and into the room. Then he allowed the door to close and he took up station next to it, his face a complete blank. He still wore his dark sunglasses and looked every bit the part of a bodyguard.

I looked around and saw a tiny man staring at first Curtis and then at me. He seemed to be going back and forth as if he didn't know who he should be watching.

"*Bonjour Monsieur*," I said.

He nodded at me. "*Bonjour*."

"Do you speak English?" I asked.

"I run an art gallery," he said. "I would be a fool not to speak the language of money."

I nodded and let my eyes take in the room. It was very large, larger than I expected it to be, and seemed to have alcoves where several pieces of framed art were hung in groupings. There were sculptures in the main room and they also seemed to be grouped as well. Whether by artist or style or period I had no idea, but it immediately made ascetic sense to my mind's eye. It was pleasing.

"Can I help you?" He had walked up to within six feet of me and stopped. He had to look way up to look in my face and it was odd to see a man as tiny and perfectly formed as he was. Think of a nine year old boy wearing a good business suit and a mustache and you would have it.

"Yes, I'm interested in oriental art, Japanese art, to be exact. I have been told you made a recent acquisition and have some to offer."

He slowly looked me up and down and two things crossed my mind simultaneously. The first was that he was most certainly gay, and second was that I would not pass muster. It was my shoes. My sport coat was fine, Brooks Brothers no less, and my jeans were pressed. But the damn shoes always reveal everything there is to know about a man and mine were just solid black Reebok running shoes. I watched him take me in and knew he would know I was not buying art wearing shoes like these.

He smiled at me, finally and I knew I was busted. But I had planned a contingency. I looked back at Curtis and then slowly at the proprietor and said, "My employers have been told you made a recent purchase and they could be very interested."

At this he smiled hugely and I knew I had done the right thing. He nodded vigorously, then came and took my arm as if he were my date to the prom.

"Come this way. Your name?"

"My name is Parker. What do I call you?"

"I am Francis Poirot, but since you are American you may call me Frankie. It is such a fun name, don't you think?" He squeezed my arm and I wanted to shake him off like an annoying white belt. I let him take me to an alcove on the far side of the room, however, and once there bent to tie my shoe. He had to let me go for that little exercise and when I stood back up I took a step back.

I looked. There were five sumi-e paintings in various forms. One was in color and four were in basic black and white. The painting in the center of the grouping was the largest and even though the lines were muted and age hung on it like a veil of moss on an old oak tree, it was clearly the masterpiece in the group. The small piece to the far left was brittle in its clarity, lines jumping off the paper like it was actually carved instead of painted, but the center piece made you sigh in wonder.

I pointed. "This is impressive. Who was the artist?"

"Kangaku Shinso, I'm certain of it. He died in the early sixteenth century. A master of the Muromachi Period, he is remembered for this type of work. I'm so certain of it I would stake my reputation on it."

"But there is no signature, nothing to identify the artist?"

"There is the stroke of his brush! That is as certain a way to identify the work as a signature or a handwriting analysis!"

He seemed suddenly angry. I thought about it for a moment and realized that it might be true, he could possess something rare and valuable, but unless he could engender belief that the artist was who he said it was, it would lose a fortune in value. I decided to go along.

"I believe you are correct." I smiled at him. "It is beyond beautiful. I think my employers would be very interested in this piece. Are these the only Japanese works you have right now?"

"Unfortunately, it is very difficult to come by now. If this was Paris and it was the turn of the last century there would be galleries filled with it. Parisians couldn't get enough of things Japanese. But now? So much was returned to the poor country after what you did to it in that horrid war…"

He paused and looked surreptitiously at me, waiting for a reaction. I have seen this many times in Europe. For a while the French, the Germans, the Italians all seemed to want Americans to apologize and grovel for the way we won the Second World War in Japan. They seemed to want to hear us deride our leaders and political system. And, unfortunately, many Americans were all too willing to go along and mumble things about how sorry they are and how much they hated Ronald Reagan, or Clinton, or whoever happened to be in power.

I refuse to play this game. I love my country and let anyone who wants to disparage it know that they are going to have a tough time getting me to say anything bad about it.

"Are you referring to the same people who bombed a country they were not at war with, and killed thousands of men sleeping in their bunks without warning?" I turned to stare right at him. "This would be the same country famous for the Bataan March of Death, or the country that brought the Chinese a million dead women, children and old people in Nanking?"

I straightened and looked intentionally down at him and in order to keep his eyes locked on mine he was forced to back up.

"I understand that there are a lot of people in the world who see things differently than I might, and those people might wish that all would be well between all our countries, as it certainly is. But don't mistake the fact that although I am representing a consortium of purchasers looking for Japanese art, that I might in any way be willing to hear someone disparage my country, any more than you would be willing to hear someone speak ill of Marseilles."

"Nooo, of course not!" He rushed over and grabbed my arm again and stood there clinging to it. "I only meant that they were so devastated... not that you did anything wrong... that..."

"How much?" I pointed.

He was instantly all business. He reached into his pocket and took out a business card and wrote a number on the back. Then he handed it to me.

I glanced at it and nodded. If it was really a Kangaku Shinso it was actually a fair price. A million above my personal budget, but for my fictitious consortium I thought it just a fine price.

I smiled at him. He smiled back and just like that we were friends again.

"I'm wondering if you might have heard a rumor about a particular piece." I glanced around the room. "It would be very special piece," I said.

He made his eyes large and doe-like. "I can't imagine. Tell me."

I think my employers will like this piece very much," I pointed at the center painting. But they specifically asked me to try and find a Miyamoto Musashi."

"*Mon Dieu*! A Musashi would be priceless! Hundreds and hundreds of millions! Is it true? Do you know where it is? Can I see it? Oh, I should like to broker that piece…"

His eyes took on a faraway look and I knew I was looking into the face of truth. If he had it he would have brought it out. No, he was not in possession of it. He actually laid his head on my bicep like we were lovers and looked up at me with fawning in his eyes.

Dead End.

It was my last hope of finding out anything pertaining to Kara's kakemono. I was done.

For form I asked to take a picture of the Kangaku Shinso and he refused.

"I have a brochure that is about to be released. You know that Marseille has been named the European Capitol of Culture for 2013? We are all thrilled. We expect to be inundated with tourists and art lovers. I will get you one. It has a picture of the Shinso. Hold on."

He left and when he came back he handed me the brochure and said, "That price will hold for seventy two hours unless someone comes into the gallery and offers full price. Then I will sell it."

His attitude was now frosty and I saw a hardness to him that I had not recognized before. He had the look of someone that might pull wings off of flies or lock a puppy in a closet and never let it out. The doe eyes now looked as if they could eat a live rat.

I turned and walked to the door. Curtis was about to open it when I stopped and turned back to Poirot.

"Can you tell me if you know of a restaurant near by that serves a good bouillabaisse?"

His face made a grimace like someone who has tasted something putrid.

"I don't like such things. I don't eat anything that ever had a mother. But, I hear that the restaurant two doors up, next to the *boulangerie*, is supposed to be famous for it."

I turned, Curtis opened the door and stepped out and then came back in and nodded. I walked out and we were free. I felt ridiculous for the charade.

The restaurant was open and doing a good business, but did have a table for us and we did not have to wait. We sat and ordered and although it took a long time for the fish stew to arrive, it was worth it. We discussed the situation and decided it was time to go back home to Orlando, Florida. It isn't the Côte d'Azur, but you can't ever discount what Dorothy said.

Chapter 28

We were driving south. I'd told Curtis that as long as we were going back I wanted to go through Toulon.

"Is there something special there?"

"No. I just can't imagine going back to Orlando and having someone ask if I had visited Toulon and saying no."

It was a town like most of the others with red tiled roofs, a port, and lots of ways to fleece tourists and locals alike. But it was really pretty. Curtis drove slowly east along the coastal highway and I watched the colors change in the Sea. We were quiet for a long time and then Curtis surprised me.

"What do you really know about the guy? Have you considered that maybe Mizushima didn't know he had a Musashi?"

"I would think that was the whole point of the theft," I said.

"But what if it wasn't?"

"What are you getting at?"

"Look, Sensei, you're a smart guy, you've been around and know a lot of things, right? So what if you walked into someone's apartment sometime and looked around, you know, just hung around for a while… Does it ever occur to you what might be valuable?"

I shook my head no. "Go on..."

"I mean, there's a dining room table and chairs and a sideboard... There's a couch and an easy chair in the living room next to a bookcase. There are paintings on the walls and a big, wide screen television with surround sound and a big stack of blue ray discs piled up there. You go over to the bookcase and see a bunch of the latest paperbacks and a couple hardbound best sellers sitting there. On the second shelf are some old books that might be something the guy bought in college, you know, like a Hemmingway, maybe *For Whom the Bell Tolls* or something. Next to it are four or five Steinbecks like they used to put out in a Book of the Month Club edition... Maybe there's Huck Finn by Mark Twain and that big book of poems everybody had to buy."

"Okay, I get your point."

"Wait, there are also a couple of those huge coffee table books on the bottom shelf and there are these paintings on the wall... There's a big oil painting with a bunch of gardens and flowers..."

"An impressionist painting."

"Right. And there are a couple water colors in a nice grouping on the other wall and by the door a little print, small, maybe twelve inches. There are even a couple small sculptures on a table by the fire place.

"Okay I get it. Make your point."

"Well, if you walked in there, what would you steal?"

I knew he was trying to show me something in a roundabout way. It was vintage Curtis, so I went along.

"I guess I'd grab the blue rays, they're always worth a few bucks. The television, the big oil painting... I don't know, I guess I'd check out the Hemmingway... If it was a first edition and if the dust jacket was in good shape it might be worth a few hundred bucks. What did I miss?"

He laughed. "Everything of value. You didn't bother to research and find out the little print on the wall was an original Renoir print. The signature is on the back. And you didn't bother to look at the Huck Finn; it's an original, first edition and signed by Sam Clemmons and worth a half million easy. Everything you took was crap. Everything else in the apartment wasn't worth two hundred bucks at a garage sale."

I watched him drive and to his credit he didn't take his eyes off the road and look in my direction.

"Okay, what you're saying is that this kid, Mizushima just knew that there was a lot of old stuff, valuable stuff, in Yamada's house and he went in, filled a couple of steamer trunks... maybe sold a piece or two to buy passage to Marseille... and then took off. He didn't really know what he had?"

"Think about it. From what you said the swords alone were worth more than the villa up there in the hills. The netsukes were owned by Tokugawa and by all rights should have been on display in the Imperial Palace. The paintings we just saw... What did he ask for that big one? A million euros? Well, who dies with all that wealth just sitting in his closet? I mean, how much could this guy have been aware of what he had?"

"You're saying he was really just a petty thief who stole what he could and fled the country and then just hid what he didn't need to sell."

"Yeah. Maybe you've been giving him too much credit."

"Annie told me that he let her play with the pretty buttons when she was a child. Good grief, think about that..."

"And if he didn't know that the old scroll was, in fact, a Miyamoto Musashi painting, he might have just left it rolled up and thrown in the back of the closet on a pile of old laundry."

I shivered.

"Just like you left the Huck Finn sitting on the bookshelf…"

"I get it, Curtis."

"And maybe, just maybe, he was still nervous about revealing what he had and where it came from, and hid it away to keep it safe, or to be a legacy for his family."

"That's giving him some credit…"

"Well, Sensei, you did say that both of the grandchildren seemed to be nice people."

I was ready to go home. I wanted to go home and leave the problem here with Kara. There was nothing else for me to do and I knew without a doubt we would never see the kakemono again. Whoever took it probably just did it on a lark, and stole the only thing in the place that looked like it had any value at all. But if it was really a sumi-e by the Sword Saint, didn't it deserve to looked for?

"I just don't know where else to look, Curtis. And besides, the thing that Kara found was probably not the Musashi… It was probably the first thing he sold when he got to France. It makes sense."

"But what if it wasn't? What if Kara actually had the Musashi?"

"Then it would be a shame if we just let it go."

I thought about what else I could do for a few miles and then had a thought. "Did I tell you about what Philippe is doing?"

"No," he said. "What's he doing? I thought he was a paleontologist or something."

"He is, something. But he's a paleontologist with a secret." I spent twenty minutes telling Curtis about the cave, the DNA profile, being part Neanderthal, and the book. Before I was done I could see that he was itching to ask questions, but that isn't the way he is. He waited until I was done and then pulled over to the side of the highway in front of a small café that looked out over the Mediterranean Sea.

"I'm thirsty," he said.

We walked through the café and out onto the back deck and sat and ordered a bottle of wine. The sun was beginning to set in the west and all the lovely topless ladies had long since fled the October chill. The color of the Sea was slate gray and when the waiter brought the wine we decided to go back inside; we live in Florida, after all.

He spent an hour asking detailed questions but kept returning to the book. He wanted to know more about the photographic program and I told him everything I could remember about it.

"What are you thinking? I asked.

"Well, it is really selfish on my part, but I'm wondering if I could get him to enhance those photographs we have of the polar region of the moon. We're spending hundreds of millions of dollars building this lunar rover to see if we can find water on the moon and maybe we could just enhance some pictures and save us all a lot of work. If it is really as good as you, anyway."

"I don't know," I said. "From what I gathered he used some special kind of light to shoot the pictures and he had this incredible camera that he got the university to fund for him. I don't know if it can process just any photograph."

Curtis was quiet while he digested what I'd told him. The waiter came back over and asked if we wanted to order anything else. Curtis shrugged. I wasn't hungry, and the man went away. This is one of the things I really like about France. You pay a little rent on a table in a café and they let you stay there all day and don't bother you.

"What kind of light?"

I thought about it. "I think he said tungsten."

"Tungsten light isn't as bright or as good as pure sunlight. Sunlight is the brightest light there is. All of my pictures were taken by the best cameras and with the best lenses that NASA has access to… I can't believe that there is anything any better on the planet. And the light is completely unfiltered by atmosphere, so it is the brightest, clearest source of light in the universe. Why wouldn't it work?"

I suddenly thought of a picture that Kara had sent me. Curtis kept talking about having Philippe enhance some of the lunar photographs and I picked up my phone and called up my email and then downloaded the files from my Yahoo account. I opened the image gallery and found the shot I wanted, then handed the phone to Curtis.

"Sunlight like this?" I asked.

The picture had been taken with the man kneeling in front of a bank of large windows. Pure sunlight streamed in and bathed the old rice paper without shadow. He looked at it and slowly began to smile. "Maybe."

"Only maybe?"

He fingered my phone and called up the properties for the picture. "I don't know who took the picture, but it's about three megabytes and should be pretty clear even at pixel level."

"But we're only interested in the area directly in front of the guy with the brush."

"So maybe about a third of the whole JPEG."

I nodded. We had a picture taken in bright sunlight with a good camera of an old scroll that was too faded to identify.

If Philippe's program could enhance it, there was at least the possibility that we could identify it and identify the artist. If we could make a positive identification then I could turn the investigation over to the French Authorities and they would certainly have the resources to hunt it down. Kara might not be happy, but at least the world would not be so much poorer for its disappearance.

"I think we need to go see Philippe. When is our plane leaving?"

"Wednesday morning at 5:00 AM," Curtis said. "We have one day."

Chapter 29

I woke early and went downstairs for a baguette and some croissants. Curtis was in the den and had the television turned on to an English speaking channel and was watching the news. I didn't disturb him. When I walked back toward the entrance of the building I saw a man approaching. It was Sean, the waiter from Ireland that I had spoken with a week before.

"Excuse me, then. But I've been wanting to apologize to you."

"Why?" I asked. I stood there with my keys in my hand and the baguette under my arm.

"I guess it could be the charm, you know. I don't often have people walk away from me. I did something I shouldn't have done and just want to set it right. I shouldn't have discussed your business with anyone else, let alone another customer. It wasn't proper, you know, and I'd just like to say I know it."

"Okay." I turned and put the key into the lock.

"Also…"

"Yes?"

"Also, I've seen Jean Claude hanging about. I've seen him come and go. He sometimes waits down there at the *Café Baton Rouge* and waits until you leave and then goes in his place."

Now I stared at him. He shrugged.

"I just felt like I owed you. Now we're even."

He walked away. I went upstairs thinking about Kara and the day she swore that she'd seen Jean Claude on the street. The man she'd seen had ducked into the small café with the big red stick on the sign.

Curtis had made coffee, lighter than I like, but still good. We ate a Continental breakfast and I told him about meeting Sean downstairs.

"Maybe he's just being polite and doesn't want you to feel you have to leave."

"Maybe he's having an affair with another woman and doesn't want to confront Kara and deal with all that."

"No offense, Sensei, but I don't know how you did it. She's a handful."

"She does have her charms. Or she did when I found them charming."

"She can still be a... well, you know."

"I do." We sat there in thought, but we couldn't come up with any reason that Jean Claude wouldn't just come upstairs, open the door, and walk in. It was his apartment after all. He owned the place, unless he was up to no good.

"Why?" Curtis asked, suddenly. "Why wouldn't he just call and say he was here and ask when you're leaving, so he knows when he can come back home. I mean, even if he was being polite. You have to live somewhere and unless he has some awful good friends to crash with... or a new love in his life, it still doesn't make any sense to spy on your own apartment. I don't like it."

I picked up my telephone and called Kara.

"*Oui?*"

"This is Parker."

"Yes, I know. I see your face in my hand."

"Sorry to call so early, but does Jean Claude know anyone in the dojo?"

"Of course, he trains here. He knows everyone in the dojo to some extent. Why? And are you calling from Florida or are you still here?"

"We leave tomorrow morning."

"Did you find my… oh, never mind. It's gone isn't it?"

"I don't know. I'm still looking for it."

"Whatever. I have to go…"

"Goodbye." I thumbed it off and looked at Curtis. "So pleasant in the morning..."

We both laughed.

"I think I'll pack this morning and get all that done early. I usually put all my dirty laundry on top where any customs agent has to paw through my dirty underwear if he wants to find my stash of Cuban cigars." He grinned at me.

"Not a bad idea."

We drifted to our respective ends of the apartment and I looked at my things and decided that tomorrow morning was good as any time. I wouldn't sleep well and knew I'd be up long before we needed to drive to the Nice airport. I'd do it then.

At ten o'clock I told Curtis that I was going to walk down to the museum and see if I could talk to Philippe Tessier.

"I'll come with."

We went down the elevator and walked the short distance to the Terra Amata museum. Curtis was fascinated and walked around the displays and exhibits while I wandered back to see if Philippe was there. A young man was working on some bones when I entered the back room and he pointed to the sign that said 'No Admittance' in four different languages.

"I'm looking for Professor Tessier," I said.

"He is not here. He is at the University today. It is the weekly staff meeting."

I thanked him and went out to the exhibits.

"It's a shame that they don't write any of the descriptions in English," he said.

"I know. I told Philippe the same thing. He took me around and told me what it all is, but don't ask because I don't remember. It's been an eventful week."

"No kidding."

"We need to go out to the University, if you want to ask him about your NASA stuff."

"Let's go."

We walked back to the apartment and went upstairs. Curtis got the car keys and I went through my papers and found the 8X10 photo of the old sensei kneeling before the kakemono that I had printed on Jean Claude's home printer. I also made sure I had a flash card with the JPEG. We went out and then spent an hour getting lost trying to find the University. There was a big difference in negotiating sidewalks or taking buses as opposed to driving on unfamiliar roads that dead ended or changed course or became one-way unexpectedly.

I showed him where we could park and then we walked past Philippe's car in his designated spot and into the big building that held the Earth Sciences. Curtis was curious about everything, which a scientist should be I suppose, and we talked all the way to Philippe's office complex.

We walked in and I nodded at several of the young people working in there and they ignored me as is the prerogative of youth. I walked back to Philippe's lab and saw Bernard Nocquet at work sorting through some files. I introduced Curtis and they spoke for few minutes about general things. I finally asked if Philippe was available.

"No, I am sorry. Today they have their weekly staff meeting. It begins at lunch and goes through five, usually. It lasts forever if you have to be there and don't want to be."

"Damn," I said. "I really need to ask him if he can look at something for me."

"Maybe you can get one of his teaching assistants to see if he can be spared for a few moments."

"Can you point one out to me?"

He waved vaguely in the direction of the front office. "They are all teaching assistants," he muttered.

I walked out to the main room and asked if anyone would be willing to go see if Professor Tessier could give me a moment of his time, but no one answered. I said it again, a little louder, and one unhappy looking boy said, "He is delivering a budget. He won't be able to see you." Then he looked back at his computer screen and I felt as isolated as a man in Death Valley at midnight.

When I returned to the back room Curtis and Bernard were hotly discussing the idea of using his program to enhance lunar photos. It seemed that Bernard liked the idea very much and thought there would be every likelihood of success.

"When can I see a sample?"

Curtis pulled out his phone and thumbed across the screen. He nodded to himself and asked if Bernard had an email address. He did and a few moments later they were both hunched over a computer and Bernard was expanding a JPEG and zooming in at the pixel level. I left them alone for about ten minutes but finally had to interrupt.

"Bernard, I know you are busy, but I wonder if you could do something for me. I am running out of time and need to see if this picture I have can be enhanced through your technique."

He looked at the computer screen and then up at me. I could tell he resented the interruption, but I also knew that Philippe would have told him I was purchasing a copy, a very expensive copy, of the book.

"All right. What do you have? Let me see it."

I handed him the 8X10 and the flash card. He glanced at it and frowned. Then he looked up at me. "What is this?"

"It's the section in the middle where it looks like a smudged piece of paper. I pointed. I need that section enhanced."

"How did you..? Oh, whatever." He shrugged and walked over to a large file cabinet in the corner. After looking in several places he finally found a file and took it out. He walked back and handed it to me.

"*Voila*." He sat and turned back to Curtis and then started manipulating the mouse again.

I was suddenly very angry with him, but opened the file to see what he had given me.

It was the photograph of the kakemono, enhanced. There was a startling 11X14 of just the kakemono section of the picture. It was brilliant in clarity and showed two peasants in conical hats bowing to the back of a samurai walking over a bridge. The sumi-e contained all the usual suspects. There was a boulder, a stream, some bamboo, and it was all right there in pristine clarity. On the right hand side of the paper there was a symbol, and I assumed it was either the date, the title of the piece of a signature. Did it say Musashi? How would I know?

And why was I holding a photo like this?

"Bernard, where did this come from?"

He looked up and acted astonished. "From me, who else? Do you see anyone else who can do this work?" He turned back to Curtis once again.

"Bernard, damn it, talk to me. Why did you enhance this photograph? Why do you have this?"

"Why else?" he said slowly standing. He was much bigger than I had thought. It happens sometimes when someone has very long legs. Sitting, they are not quite as impressive. But if he thought he could intimidate me he was mistaken. He still had to look up at me.

"Can you explain to me why you have this?"

"Professor Tessier asked me to do it." He crossed his arms and looked at the ceiling.

"But, when?"

He sat back down and closed the file he was working on with Curtis and then called up another folder. He checked the properties and said, "August the fifteenth."

It was the last week of October. Philippe had seen this over two months ago. Philippe had known.

I felt like a bloody fool.

Chapter 30

"Philippe asked you to enhance this photograph two months ago?"

"Yes. So what?"

Curtis suddenly looked up and realized everything in a single instant.

"I see. Did he explain why he needed you to do it?"

"We were developing the program. It was a challenge... the original as you know is dreadful. I was very pleased it turned out so well."

"Did Philippe say anything about the enhanced picture?"

Now Bernard looked at me with genuine curiosity. "Is something wrong? You seem upset with this. I thought you wanted it done and now I hand it to you, it is done, and you are not so happy." He eyed me uncertainly.

"No. Quite the contrary, you have cleared up several mysteries. Thank you. Can I have this?"

"Oh, no." He reached out and put the photograph back in the folder and walked it back to the file cabinet.

I felt the heat rising again. "Would you please make me one?"

"I cannot make one like that without the use of the printer and that takes weeks to schedule. And the price would be ridiculous."

"Don't you have a printer here?"

"We have a normal laser printer, but the photo would not look like that…"

"Would it show all the detail?"

"Yes, sure. It would just be a normal photograph of the image, though, nothing so…"

"Fine. Would you please print a couple for me in the largest format the laser printer has?"

He turned to the computer, punched several keys and then sat back. "Are you satisfied?"

I offered both hands, palm up.

"*Mon Dieu…*" He got up and walked out of the room. In ten seconds he was back and handed me two 11X14 pages with the picture printed on it. He was right, these were nothing like the original, they were flat, dull and lifeless, but they were also clear and crisp and I could see all the detail, just fine.

"Thank you, Bernard. I mean that. This has been a great help to us."

He seemed mollified. "Well, we should always help, I suppose…"

"Will you see Philippe today?" I asked.

"No. I will finish my filing and then I am on holiday for the rest of the week. I leave as soon as I am done." He smiled.

"Okay, well, just mention that I was here the next time you see the good professor, okay?"

"*Certainement.*"

I nodded to Curtis and he told Bernard he would be in touch about working with NASA. I could tell they were both very pleased with the idea. We left and I paused at the door.

"*Au revoir*," I said. Then we walked out of the office and down the long hallway and out to the car. I opened the passenger door and slid in and waited for the anger to subside a bit.

"Son of a bitch," I hissed.

"It was Philippe all along," said Curtis. "He stole it. He must have sold it, too."

"I feel like such a complete fool," I said. "He took me everywhere and we laughed and talked about all kinds of things. I thought we were becoming friends."

"What does the mafia say? Keep your friends close, and keep your enemies closer? He was behind the whole thing."

"I think that was Sun Tzu, actually, but Don Corleone is good enough for me. Is there any other explanation? He knew what the kakemono was, right?" I thought about it for a minute. "Well, wait. What is it? He might have done it innocently you know... it was just a smudged piece of paper... Is it possible he didn't make the connection? Or is it possible this is not the Musashi? It's just a pretty picture as far as I can tell."

"But once he found out it was something like this he should have told someone."

"Told them what?" I dug into my briefcase and got out my laptop. I googled Miyamoto Musashi and then called up images, but after a few minutes I began to get frustrated.

"Here," I said. "You're a rocket scientist and a computer nerd. Find Musashi's signature and then compare it to this." I handed him one of the pictures and then leaned my head back on the headrest in the Volvo. I closed my eyes and let myself calm down and tried to use my brain for a change.

I listened to Curtis click keys and then wait and then hit more key strokes. After ten minutes I opened my eyes and saw he was frowning deeply.

"I can't make anything out. I don't know what I'm looking at and haven't got a clue what to look for. This is ridiculous." He turned to look at me and said, "Sorry Sensei, this is such a piece of shit I just can't use it. Let's go back to the apartment and I'll try my Apple."

"You got a problem with my Acer?" I asked. "I paid almost two hundred dollars for this piece of shit."

"You get what you pay for…"

"I know," I sighed. "It's just for travel and for emails and surfing. You know, call up the news and weather… nothing serious."

"And you do know there's a difference between Google and research, right?"

It was my turn to look at him.

"Okay, sorry. That was uncalled for. But look, I don't know about this stuff, signatures in kanji and what not. I don't even know what to look for."

"Well, damn Curtisn, isn't it a shame we just happen to have access to a native speaker of Japanese who also just happens to read and write all that kanji and stuff…"

He looked shocked. "Wait a minute. I haven't talked to my wife in two months. She left me, remember?"

"She was freaked out, you ass! She left you to get your attention! You almost got cut in half and you refused to talk about it with her. From what I hear you refused to do anything but pass the time of day with her."

"You don't understand, Sensei. She wanted me to talk about my feelings. My feelings! She wanted me to say how I felt, how I feel… Crap, I don't know how I feel other than pissed off that I didn't manage to do a decent tenkan and take the sword away from that asshole and shove it up his butt. I'm mad at myself for not being better. I'm mad at myself for not throwing the bastard off the top of the parking garage like you did. I can't say that to her. I don't do feelings very well."

I let the silence settle for a bit and then turned to him. "You should have just said what you just did. She would have understood that Curtis. You were quite eloquent just then." I paused, considered, and then continued. "She's your wife. I suspect she loves you and would have been proud to have seen you angry with your inability to kill. She would have been proud of you if you had clawed his heart out of his chest and then eaten it, or made him eat it. She's your wife and wives have the unbelievable ability to see good in their husbands when it is almost never there. They have the ability to deny all the horrible shit that's obvious to every other woman on the planet. They have the ability to forgive anything. They aren't like us. They can do things that we never could and believe things we never would. They are better than us, and much smarter, and, well, just better. She's your wife and you need to call her and ask for her help."

I waited a full ten seconds and then said, "Please."

He sighed and nodded his head. "Okay. Let's go back to the apartment and let me make up a folder of images and documents and then I'll send it to her and then call to make sure she understands that it's business and that we need it right away."

He almost seemed relieved. He almost seemed to like the idea that he had an excuse to call her.

Men are so pathetic, I thought. We are willing to die for our country, willing to die to save the life of someone we wouldn't speak to civilly in passing; we are willing to suffer the most unbelievable anguish and suffering and hardship to achieve a goal that is meaningless… but good God, don't make us talk about our feelings.

Chapter 31

"I want to go back and talk to Philippe," I said. "I want to ask him face to face what he's done and why."

"Okay. Give me one more minute and then I'll send this and call Mariko. She can look at it while we talk and I explain everything. If she can't give us an answer right away it probably isn't going to matter because we are going to be flying out of here in about thirteen hours."

"Okay," I said. "Do it."

He bent over the keyboard and I walked into the kitchen. I picked up my phone and went into the bedroom to give him a little privacy. After a few minutes I heard the muted tones of a one sided conversation and then I heard a door close. He had gone into the sitting room where Jean Claude presumably watched television.

Ten minutes later we met in the kitchen.

"Well?" I asked.

"She says that the signature, well, it's really a chop, or a seal… something like a rubber stamp we might use today, but back then they carved them out of ivory or bone or something…

"Okay, I get it."

"Well, she said that if it's not a forgery, then it's probably a Musashi. The chop matches."

"A forgery? Christ on a crutch, can this thing get any more screwed up? A forgery?"

216

"She said that there have been dozens of hoaxes and forgeries of not just Musashi, but a lot of the old stuff. She said finding a real Musashi would be tantamount to finding a painting by Leonardo da Vinci or Botticelli... The time is about the same. Imagine what an oil painting by da Vinci would be worth. People do lots of bad things for money."

"Don't I know it. Okay, let's assume that this is real and that we have finally identified the piece as being the stolen Musashi that belonged to Yamada and was brought here by Mizushima fifty years ago. Okay?"

"Okay."

"Show me the chop."

Curtis took a pen and circled the identifying chop and then showed me two other pictures on his laptop that had the same thing. I looked and had a very hard time seeing it, but eventually a few shapes and marks seemed to make sense and it did seem to be the same. It was almost like a picture window that had little up-curved swirls at the edges.

"Okay. I think I could sell that to a French cop. Let's go talk to Philippe and see if it's gone or if he still has it and if he does would he consider returning it so we can get it to the right people. This needs to be returned to Japan."

Curtis hesitated and then looked at me. "We aren't going to get in a pitched battle are we? I don't think I'm up for another fight."

"Curtis, if it even begins to look like there might be conflict I don't want you involved. You've done enough for a lifetime. Just turn the car around and get back here and head for the airport. Got it?"

"That makes me feel like I'd be abandoning you. I can't do that."

"How many stitches did you get? A hundred? Two hundred? How many months to heal a cut by a samurai sword that should have cut you in half? Don't give me any crap about abandoning me. If it looks hinky, just take off."

He looked at his shoes for a moment and then nodded his head. "Okay."

"Okay. Good. Let's go, then."

He grabbed the keys and we made the now familiar drive to the university in a misting rain that seemed to be blowing up from the south across the Mediterranean Sea. It was chilly and damp and we were too late. I saw Philippe drive out across the parking lot from a block away and told Curtis to chase him down.

"A Frenchman?" he asked.

"Do your best. I'll try and keep him in sight. You just drive."

The Volvo took the corner faster than I would have liked and skidded a bit, but Curtis was able to handle the big car and for a while it looked like we were gaining on Philippe. He had us by at least three blocks and was driving, typically, like a bat out of hell.

"Do you think he knows we're after him?"

"I doubt it," I said. "This is how he drives. I had to close my eyes a couple times when we headed into the mountains. He scared the crap out of me." I watched him turn his car into a narrow street and Curtis had to slow down to a far greater extent to make the turn. Philippe was disappearing over a rise and I lost sight of him.

"Just keep going," I said.

We crested the rise and saw that the road made a sharp, hairpin turn and then headed directly into a tree lined boulevard that was separated by ancient chestnuts. I saw Philippe's car between two of the giants and told Curtis to turn left. We followed much more slowly then as the traffic thickened. We were trying to keep a distance that left us a few cars back, but it was vulnerable to a surge through a red light. I saw his tail lights come on several times and realized he was looking for a parking place.

"Be ready to stop and let me out. I think he's going to park. Ease over to the outside lane. If he parks go past him and then when I say, just stop. I'll jump out. You circle the block as long as it takes."

"Got it."

We watched and I saw his brake lights flare and then he stopped and reversed into a tiny spot I couldn't believe he would fit into, but a nudge of the car in front and a harder nudge of the car in back and then he was climbing out. We drove past and I looked away and then told Curtis to let me out.

He slammed on the brakes and I stepped out into the rain. It was coming harder now and it was cold and bitter in the darkening sky. Philippe was nowhere to be seen. I stepped under a chestnut tree and out of the misting rain and waited. I did not want to let him see me coming. I just wanted to step in front of him and ask him why, and see the look on his face.

I felt so strangely betrayed. It was personal now. I don't make friends easily and it had seemed like we were actually doing just that. There had been a mutual respect, I thought. We had shared some good dinners and wine and had laughed a lot. And he had shared his greatest secret with me.

Keep your enemies closer…

I finally gave up expecting to see him and started to walk the street and look into the different businesses. He might have been in the clothing store in a dressing room, but I doubted it. He was not in the *Fromagerie Unique*, The cheese shop had but one counter and it was occupied by

French women discussing the right level of ripeness, I imagined. He was not in the law office, it was closed. I passed a café and saw what appeared to be his head at a table with two other men and then recognized both of them simultaneously. Damn, damn, and damn, again.

Jean Claude was standing at the high top table and was waving his hand in front of his face. He held a cigarette and I could see the flaming end leave tracers in the air as he talked. Ken was a head shorter than Jean Claude, but he was by far the most serious of the three. Though shorter, he seemed formidable in a undefined way, the way that some politicians and judges do, internal confidence, something… Between them Philippe almost seemed broken. He slumped at the table and it almost seemed like he would collapse if the table did not prop him up.

A waiter brought them a bottle of wine and three glasses and Jean Claude poured without ceasing to talk. He kept his rant going and both of his companions listened and occasionally Ken nodded his head and sometimes Philippe turned to stare at him and then look back at the table top.

I eased out of the light and stepped quickly across the wide street and once again under a huge chestnut tree. Rain was dripping through the canopy now, and though it did not do a lot to keep me dry. It did offer darkness where the street lights could not penetrate the trunks and leaves. I waited and watched.

Curtis drove past a half dozen times and finally I called him on my smart phone and told him what the situation was. I suggested he find a parking place further up the block and wait for my call. I told him not to answer when I rang, just get the car into traffic and come pick me up. We might be in a hurry. I let him know where I was staked out and eventually saw him drive past again and look in my direction. Then I quit thinking about him.

It took nearly two hours, but eventually I watched Ken walk out the door, turn up his collar and flip his scarf around his neck and then saunter down the boulevard in the direction that would lead him to the main drag and the tram line. Philippe came next with Jean Claude right behind him and although Philippe indicated his car at the curb Jean Claude shook his head adamantly and stalked off. It's the only word that fits.

I sprinted across the street and Philippe was completely unaware of my coming until I put a hand on the car door and stopped him opening it. It jerked out of his hands and slammed shut in the steady rain. He turned and stared at me outraged, but hesitated and then smiled when he recognized me. It was a good effort, too.

"Sensei! I thought you would be back in the Florida sunshine by now." He tried to smile bigger, but failed and then I saw the smile fade. "Why are you here? It is quite a coincidence, no?"

I took him firmly by the arm. He began to resist as I pulled him under the restaurant canopy. He jerked his arm twice and then I spun him around and looked him in the eye and said, "Really?"

I felt all resistance go out of him. "I know I can't fight you. Yes, but please let me go."

I did.

"What do you want, Sensei?" He sounded exhausted.

"I want to know why, Philippe. That's all. I just want to know why."

"Why?" He gave me that Gallic smile of perplexed amusement meant to disarm, but tonight it only gave his face a grimace of terror and useless, forlorn hope. He spread his hands in front of him and said it again. "Why?"

I stared at him. I gave him nothing. Finally he leaned against the building and said quietly, "I have nothing left."

"Bullshit. You're going to be the most famous paleontologist in the world very soon. Don't tell me that's nothing."

"When your wife leaves you... and your daughter asks for money for school and you have none to give... When you must borrow from friends and there is no hope of ever getting enough money to publish this book..."

"Forget the damn book, Philippe. Just call a press conference and give away the damn cave and you'll get so many requests for guest lectures that you won't know what to do with all the money."

"You don't know how it works, here. Without the book my part in the discovery will disappear. Without the complete documentation of the cave, with my name in print all over it there will be a president's name or a..."

"Yeah, we've been through all of this. You stole from your sensei. You stole from your dojo."

He did that damned puff of air thing, blowing it out of his mouth like a fart half formed and it made me furious.

"You sold a world class treasure to gangsters!"

"I needed the money!"

"Is it gone?" I hissed.

He looked at me and I saw him try to compose himself. "Yes, it is gone," he challenged.

He was lying.

"Why are you meeting Jean Claude and Ken Poullard?"

"I..."

"And don't bullshit me, Philippe. I have enough evidence that you stole and deciphered the kakemono that I can go to the police and get a monster of an investigation started. I want the truth. I want the Musashi. I want it to go back to Japan where it belongs. I'm not going to stop until this whole thing gets dragged into the light of day."

He stared up into my face for a long moment and then seemed to deflate. "Come…"

He walked a few steps to an outside table. The canopy kept the rain at bay and a wave of my hand stopped the waiter. No one wanted to sit outside on such a rainy, bitter night and I was sure we would not be bothered. We sat.

"When I took the photographs of Tamura Sensei painting the Aikido kanji I did not think anything about the original picture we covered up. Please believe that. It was only when Bernard was showing me the amazing work his new photographic process was capable of that I remembered the old sumi-e. I asked him to see what he could do with it. I was innocent. It meant nothing and there was no ill will involved."

"Go on."

"I saw the picture when he was finished… I suppose you have as well?"

I nodded.

"Of course, I realized it was special, but not how special. I asked Jean Claude to look at it and to show it to Kara Sensei, but he said he didn't know anything about Japanese art, but would take it to Japan. He was leaving in a week or so for his annual time spent at his corporate headquarters in Tokyo. He told me not to say anything until he got back; we would keep it as a surprise for her."

"Some surprise, all right."

"Sensei, please, it was not like that… At least not at first."

"Whatever," I said. I couldn't keep the disgust out of my voice.

"Jean Claude took a photograph of the sumi-e to Japan and asked around at his company headquarters and someone there told him it was a Musashi. He got very excited, but Jean Claude realized the immensity of his mistake and convinced him that it was only a print. But apparently Ken found out. Jean Claude had asked a number of people and the old man who had identified it had talked. Ken was there at the same time and he knew Jean Claude... They are both from Nice, after all. They discussed it and it became apparent to Ken that the kakemono came from his family collection. He became furious and demanded it be returned to him."

"Money does bad things to people."

"Eventually he threatened to take it from Jean Claude by force. This was about the time that they were going to return to France. He called me and told me that I needed to get the kakemono and keep it safe. He said he was worried that it would be stolen by gangsters from Japan. I asked him to tell me what it was and when he did I couldn't believe it. All my problems would go away. They would disappear. I would be able to do exactly what I needed. My wife would return. My daughter could go to any school she desired, anywhere. I was saved."

"Not quite, buddy. It didn't belong to you."

"No." He shook his head.

I waited.

"I stole it."

"I know."

"It would have been stolen by the Yakuza if I hadn't."

"You could have turned it over to the Japanese Embassy. End of story."

He looked up into my eyes and for the first time that evening I saw the sad, sorry look of true honesty on his face.

"I couldn't. I needed the money."

"Who did you sell it to?"

"It was the Yakuza. But they threatened to steal it if we did not turn it over to them for cash. They threatened to kidnap and kill. They threatened Kara Sensei and Ken's sister, Anastasia. We were frightened. We are still frightened. I felt we were up against the wall. You say this?"

"Yeah," I said. "We say our backs are up against the wall, too. So you gave it to them."

He hesitated slightly. I'm not sure that anyone who has not spent thousands of hours on an Aikido mat would have detected the hesitation, but that is what we train for. We reach out with ki and try to feel the sudden impulse that spells attack or misdirection. I'm not sure even Opie Taylor would have felt it, but I did.

"Yes," he said. "It is gone."

"And now you're rich. How does that feel?"

"I am sick. I tried to make the others understand we should not do this, but how can one convince others when he cannot convince himself?" He spread out his hands.

"Okay," I said. It stood up and walked away. I walked down the block and saw Curtis sitting in the Volvo and walked past it and then cut across the street and stepped into shadows. I watched Philippe stand up and slowly climb into his car. Once he had pulled the door shut I stepped from the shadows and across the sidewalk and opened the car door.

"Get ready to follow that lying, thieving bastard."

Curtis slipped the car in gear and waited, watching the rear view mirror. "Tell me when, this might get dicey."

"Okay, there he goes. Don't lose him. I think this is our last chance."

Chapter 32

Curtis pulled the big car out into the evening traffic. The wheels spun and then grabbed the wet surface. I watched Philippe drive doggedly through the rainy night and tried to keep us back far enough that he would not make us, but close enough that we would not be caught by surprise. After a few minutes it became apparent he was just driving and I suspected he was going home. I had never been there, but he had told me that he lived in a modern area of Nice in a modern building. He finally slowed and then turned into a small parking lot that had a gate that opened and closed with a card or something that he used through the open window.

We slowed and I indicated that Curtis should wait, so he doused the headlights and we watched Philippe park and enter a building with a glass foyer and tile sills on the windows. It looked to be from the 1950s and for this part of Nice that would have counted as modern. I assumed he was home.

"Park wherever you can, but let's try to be somewhere where we can follow him whichever way he goes."

He did. He parked on a street that gave us a clear view of the front of the building, but that was on a tee to the main street. Whichever way Philippe drove we could follow without problem.

"What are we doing?"

I spent ten minutes telling Curtis everything we had said.

"Then it's over."

"No. He hasn't delivered it yet."

"But you said he told you…"

"He was lying. He isn't very good at it either."

"Well," Curtis said and looked at me. "He did a pretty good job on you all last week."

It was my turn to slump. "He did."

"What are we going to do?"

"We are going to wait until he leaves and then we are going to follow him; and then I am going to take the damned kakemono away from him and then we are going to turn it over to the police."

"What if he doesn't leave and it turns into 2:00 or 3:00 AM? Are we going to get our stuff and leave France?"

"Yes."

He seemed relieved.

We waited.

An hour ticked by and we just sat and watched.

Around 9;00 o'clock Curtis asked me if I thought it possible that Philippe might have the Musashi in his apartment.

"I've been considering it, but I don't think so."

"Why?"

"The Yakuza thugs have been going all over looking for it. I don't think they care if they steal it, kill a dozen people for it, or pay for it."

"Really?"

"Why would they care?"

"Why not?"

"Because if they kill for it they just do. If they steal it, they get it for nothing. And if they buy it… What can they be paying? A million euros? Five million? Again, it's nothing compared to what it's really worth, so in essence they're stealing it even then. No, I think that whoever is the boss of this operation has just told his minions to get it at whatever cost."

"Minions?"

"Whatever. You know what I mean. His men, his posse, his under lords, his gang, his…"

"I get it."

We were quiet for a while, but Curtis never shuts his brain off. "Where do you think it is?"

"I don't know, but I have some ideas."

"Where would you hide something priceless from someone who wanted to take it from you?"

I looked at him. "Really?"

"Yeah. Where?"

I thought about it and could think of a lot of places. I could also think of a lot of scenarios that could be turned back on me if it did not go right. "A bank safe deposit box," I finally said.

He shrugged. "They could force you to give them the key."

"At the University in his private offices."

"Same deal."

"I'd mail it to myself."

That turned his head.

"I'd pick a post office that was not too far away from my regular post office, say Winter Park, and then I'd send it to myself at that post office to General Delivery."

"General Delivery?"

"Yeah. It isn't very common anymore with all post offices making you come up with all sorts of identification and proof of address just to get a P.O. Box, but you can still send stuff to general delivery and they put all the stuff into a secure room until you pick it up."

"How do you get it?"

"You just walk in and say you are expecting a package. They ask for identification and then they go back and see if there's anything there for you. Unless you told a bunch of people that you did it, who would know? You pick a post office and then use it. There are nearly fifty thousand post offices in the United States."

"That's genius."

"I used to like to send packages to a friend in Orlando. This is years ago. We would choose a post office and she would go pick them up."

"Why didn't you just send them to her house?"

"I think we were afraid her husband would object."

He waited a second and then we both laughed.

"You, Sensei, are a scoundrel."

"I've always thought so."

We laughed again. It was good seeing Curtis laugh. It had been a long time.

"There he is."

I looked up and saw Philippe walking across the street and going to his car.

Curtis waited until he had gotten in and closed the door before he started the Volvo. We watched him ease out and turn left toward the heart of the city and we followed for a few blocks without lights. Then, as we approached a business district Curtis finally fell behind another car and switched his headlights on. We continued to follow Philippe through the rain soaked, dark night for ten minutes and I realized we were getting very close to the Port district where Jean Claude's apartment was. He went through Garibaldi Square and then turned right at Rue Cassini and followed it past Saint Sebastian until it dead ended at Rue de l'Hotel des Postes. We watched him park and then go into the large building.

It took twenty minutes but eventually he walked out carrying a thick mailing tube that was about sixteen inches long. I started to get out. I had decided to just take it from him, no bullshit, no excuses. There would be no beating around the bush; I was just going to take it. But then the damn commuter tram came gliding up and stopped right in front of us, and by the time it had gone, he was gone.

Yeah, I'm a fucking genius.

Chapter 33

"Drive!"

"Where?"

"Go back the way we came. Jean Claude lives less than a mile from here. There was a reason he chose this spot. Backtrack!"

He did. We drove all the way to Jean Claude's apartment and then I told him to turn around and go back up Rue Cassini. The only place they could be going was the big square. Garibaldi Square was perfect. Many roads enter it and there would be many escape routes. Rue Cassini was a straight shot.

It is a narrow street with shops at the very edge of the sidewalk and it enters right into Garibaldi Square. There are restaurants and shops offering clothing, electronics, locksmiths, and grocery; all sorts of things that everyone needs on a daily basis, but as you get closer to the square the restaurants become more common. Once you get there, it seems that besides the big Monoprix grocery across the square it is surrounded by restaurants and hundreds of milling locals and tourists.

But not tonight. Tonight it was dark and foggy and silent. The rain fell from the sky with an almost mystical gentleness. I asked Curtis to stop and park nearly a block back and then looked at him and said, "Remember what I told you. If it hits the fan, go."

I got out and walked slowly, doing my best to stay silent. A closed *boulangerie* had left their canopy open; I stopped and hid in the deep shadow. After moments holding my breath I moved on and found another dark recess and again waited. I kept moving. I stopped and used the tiger walk to cross grates and rough place and eventually found myself in the square itself, in the dark hidden recesses of a restaurant that only served breakfast and lunch and stacked its tables and chairs on the covered patio.

Streetlights made crescents of diamonds falling from the sky and I watched as a man got out of a dark sedan parked on the far side of the square. He walked into the middle of the arena and suddenly I saw another dome light flash as yet another man opened the door of his car. I heard an automobile start and then saw Philippe's car drive into Garibaldi Square from the Avenue de la Republique. He stopped in the rain and all three men converged and spoke in the glow of the headlights.

Jean Claude was more animated than before. Ken was as quiet and assured. Philippe looked as if he wanted to run away and leap from a bridge and I didn't give a damn about any of them. All I wanted was to get my hands on the sumi-e and then give it to the Japanese Embassy and then get the hell off this damn continent and go home to the stinking, alligator infested swamps of Central Florida.

It was becoming a matter of perspective.

I saw headlights enter the square from the far side near the Monoprix grocery. It looked like a Mercedes sedan and I knew it was the Yakuza. Would they just step out of the car and shoot them all? I could think of a dozen reasons why they should. It made all sorts of sense. Shooting them down would make all their problems go away as far as identification and tracking and destination. And yet I thought about it. Could I identify them if I even wanted? I had fought them and been up close and personal. What could I say? They were Japanese with tattoos.

And what had Curtis told me? Guns were virtually nonexistent in Europe. Oh, they had shotguns and rifles but those were closely monitored for hunters. Handguns were so closely guarded that they existed only in movies. I remember when a few French students came over to my dojo for a seminar. When we had brought out a few handguns after class they had been stunned. They just couldn't believe it when we told them that many Americans had them. We offered to take them to a shooting range or up into the big national park at Ocala so they could try them and they had enthusiastically agreed. It had been a highlight of their American adventure.

Or maybe the Yakuza would just pay them off. It would certainly be quieter. I moved up past the tables and stacks of chairs as close as I could get and still be in shadow. The Mercedes inched closer and then stopped perhaps ten yards from the front grill of Philippe's car. The four headlights pointing at each other turned the area between the vehicles into stage lighting for a rock show. Philippe and Jean Claude were lit up so brightly I could see the color of their eyes from a hundred feet away.

The trunk lid popped up and then four men opened doors and climbed out of the car. They were my old friends. The small, portly man wearing a bandage across his nose and a pork pie hat walked to the trunk and lifted out a suitcase. The other three walked slowly toward Philippe and his crew and then slowly, gradually, moved in a semicircle around them. The leader threw his cigarette on the cobblestones and then took the suitcase. He set it down and said something to

Ken, then held out something small, a key perhaps, and indicated he wanted the tube that Philippe was holding.

Ken turned to Philippe and motioned for the tube. He held out his hand. Philippe started to hand it to him when I stepped out of the shadow and sprinted the hundred feet and slammed into Jean Claude, sending him sprawling. I snatched the tube from Philippe's hand and saw that he was so frightened he was practically in shock. Ken screamed at me to give it to him and then the Yakuza had me surrounded. I watched the leader reach into his coat pocket and take out a knife. It flicked in the blazing light from the headlamps and glittered from rain drops in seconds. Around me I heard knives snicking open and turned, backing away from them and then circling to keep them all in sight.

It's been years since I last read *The Book of Five Rings*, Miyamoto Musashi's masterwork on martial art strategy. But I must have read it cover to cover a dozen times when I was studying it because whole passages are committed to memory. In *The Water Book* he has a small section titled *There Are Many Enemies* and it describes how to fight multiple attackers. It is the basis for all Aikido *randori*. Musashi describes chasing the enemy until they are in a line and then fighting them one on one and never letting them find a position where two or more can can attack you simultaneously.

I did this now. Using the tube I smacked Ken across the bridge of the nose and saw him drop. I stepped over him and launched myself at the leader of the pack. That is always a good strategy as it sometimes undermines the will of underlings to see their leader fall. He was careful. He had been knocked unconscious by me once before and was aware he was dealing with an accomplished martial artist. He backed up and I stepped to his right lining up the others behind him. Then I attacked. It was pure *irimi* and I didn't think at all. I just entered and waited for his response.

He thrust the knife at my solar plexus with a powerful *tsuki* but I didn't hesitate. I thought of Musashi again, and maybe he was guiding me in some bizarre bond of kindred spirits, because I used *the Fire and Stones Cut* to deflect his attack. Flicking the tube up with my left hand and deflecting the tip of the blade I launched a fist directly to the center of his face and drove off my rear foot with all my power and all the ki I could dredge up from where the earth joins the center of the universe.

The sounds of breaking bones filled the square. He went down and did not move, but I continued as if I had met only air and swept the second man around in a massive *ikkyo* that took him completely off his feet. He flew through the air at the end of my right hand until his head met the bumper of the Mercedes. It dented and he went limp. Then, before I could turn I was slammed into the grill and I saw a hand slip under and around and knew I was going to get cut. He was trying to get to my throat. But the other gangster interrupted the stroke, slamming in to me as well and then I saw the knife in front of my face and grabbed it and reversed.

I had the small man in *sankyo* and turned hard with both my elbows locked to my sides. I broke his arm. I actually felt the bone let go and heard his scream, but I did not let go. The other gangster backed off and I knew then it was over. In the second it would take to recover my *ma ai* he would have the knife in my heart. There was just no option. I saw everything slow down then, saw the rain freeze-framed in its trajectory, saw Philippe's face frozen in a mask of terror, saw the Yakuza draw back and begin his killing thrust.

My knees were locked to the fender of the Mercedes and my way out was blocked by the man I held. I saw blackheads and acne across the attacker's face and smelled tobacco, whisky and fear as time stopped and then I saw him lifted into the air and watched as he flew past me and shattered the windshield of the big car. He lay across the shattered glass and blood began to flow down his chest and onto the hood. I turned to the man I was holding and drove my elbow into his face. I did it almost casually and he did not even try to avoid it or flinch out of the way. He fell.

Then I became aware of the booming echoes of the monster handgun that had saved my life. I knew the sound. I knew it very well. It was a .44 magnum and I also knew who had fired the bullet. I turned and looked down the alley, but there was no one there. I looked across at the other streets that entered into Garibaldi Square but they were also deserted. There was only Philippe standing and looking at me. There was Ken kneeling, holding his nose and Jean Claude walking quickly away.

I leaned against the side of the big car and looked up into the sky. A huge weight pushed against my heart, but a great peace and calm stole over me. Diamonds fell and scattered across the cobbled stones of the vast arena. The tube that held the priceless piece of art had stayed together. I held it to my chest with crossed arms. The sounds of broken bodies trying to hold on to consciousness and life were all around me. I heard the sounds of two engines running and music playing softly somewhere.

Once again I looked to the sky and heard in the distance the sirens of the French police driving through the night to the sounds of a battle, and a gun, and men dying. I waited. I had all the time in the world now. Rain fell in sheets and glittered in the street lights and in the headlights and in the soft light falling from the third story windows that surround the square. The light turned the rain drops into jewels cascading from the heavens. The sight of diamonds falling fascinated me and I couldn't stop looking even as the diamonds turned to sapphires.

Chapter 34

They kept at me for three days. They brought in different investigators and different interpreters. After the first day the local police were replaced by more sophisticated men in better suits. They asked me to repeat it all again. I did. I told them everything. I held back nothing. I told the truth. It is almost impossible to be caught up in a lie when you stick to the truth.

The third day they were gone and a new breed of investigator appeared. Interpol. They were joined by men from the French Embassy and then the Japanese Embassy and then the United States Embassy. They tried to make me feel like a criminal. They tried to make me out to be an art thief. They called me a liar and wanted to know who my accomplice was and how did he manage to disappear with the gun? They assumed I wanted the Musashi for myself and only intended to take it for myself.

I stuck to my story. I named names. I got everyone involved from Kara to Annie to Bernard. It was Kara who told them we had discussed returning it to the Japanese. She told them that once she found out what it was she had begged me, a famous American private investigator, to help so she could return it. She played the part well. They called Orlando and spoke with police there.

Yes, they knew me. Yes, I was respectable, to a certain extent, anyway. Yes, I was a private investigator. No, I had never been arrested or indicted or been in prison. As for my being an honorable man, well, at least one homicide investigator spoke up for me.

On the morning of the fourth day I was unceremoniously rousted from fitful sleep, still at the table I had been sitting at for eighty hours, and hauled out to a waiting police car. They drove me to the Nice airport in the early morning dark. There, I was walked up to the open doors of an Air France flight and escorted aboard. To my surprise I was taken to the left, up towards first class.

"You made a huge mistake in that you broke many French laws. People died. Guns were fired. Men are in hospital. It is an international story. An amazing art treasure... well, you know how it is."

I looked at the man who was now taking the handcuffs off my wrists.

"But the Japanese Embassy believes you were trying to do the right thing and return a national treasure. There is a man who spoke up for you. Apparently a well known man, and a man of reasonable power. He is the head of the school, this Aikido, yes? He said you were known to him, a professor. The Japanese have a great deal of respect for these kinds of things."

I didn't have a clue. I was exhausted and sleep-deprived and hungry.

The French policeman shrugged. I silently hoped it would be the last shrug I saw for a long time.

"Well, it must have carried weight. They believed you and felt you should return home in comfort. If I may be so bold; it would be a good idea if you stayed away from France for a while."

Not a problem, I thought.

He left. The stewardess walked up the aisle and stopped beside me. She was very pretty and I thought in my tiredness and relief that she looked like an angel. She asked me if I would like a preflight glass of champagne.

"Leave the bottle, if you don't mind," I said.

Chapter 35

I managed to get from the international terminal at JFK to Delta in time to see my plane roaring down the runway. Typical. By the time I finally got to Orlando it was dark and rush hour was long past. I took a cab. It was an extravagance for me, the bus runs a block from my house, but I didn't care. I just wanted it all to be over and to be back in my little Florida cracker house with my dogs and my dojo.

When the driver let me out I stood there feeling perplexed. Lights were on and there were many cars in the driveway and in the parking area and then I realized it was Friday night and the last class was still going on. I had to go back to the dojo and find my spare set of keys in order to unlock my house.

Curtis nodded at me from the mat when I walked in and I quickly shook my head no, and walked through the dojo to my office. He would have stopped the class and had everyone turn and bow and I just didn't want the attention.

The house was warm and smelled musty. Air conditioning and fans quickly overcame the considerable ability of Florida to decompose anything left too long unattended. After a while, and about two glasses of Gosling's Black Seal rum, I heard cars leaving. I tried to unwind. I was exhausted and jet lagged and wanted to go to bed, but I knew I would talk to Curtis before I could do that.

Eventually the last car pulled out of the driveway and I heard him knock and call to me. "Sensei?"

"C'mon in."

"Wait."

He left and returned a few minutes later and I saw he was carrying my beautiful leather shoulder bag/brief case and my suitcase.

"I hope I got everything."

"I can't believe you went back and got it at all," I said.

He held up his hands and I snapped, "Don't shrug!"

We both laughed. I spent the next half hour telling him everything and he told me that he had driven away as soon as he saw me surrounded by the Yakuza. He said, quite sorrowfully, that he felt bad doing it. I told him he had done the right thing. He had gotten my briefcase and laptop. Hell, he was my hero.

"What about my phone..."

"It's in the shoulder bag, in the side pocket."

"God, that's wonderful. Do you know how long it would take me to program another one? Did you have any trouble getting away?"

"None. I just went back to Jean Claude's and packed in about two minutes. Then I drove carefully to the airport and turned in the car and by the time everything was done I only had about two hours to kill before the five o'clock plane to New York. Once I got on and the damn thing took off, I let out a big sigh of relief. You know, right up until the moment that plane left I was convinced you were going to walk through the door and get on board.

"I almost didn't get out at all."

We were quiet and then he stood and said, "We can talk more later. You look exhausted."

"How are things with you?" I asked. "Have you seen Mariko?"

He nodded and said, "She moved back in yesterday. We're going to try to make it work."

"Good."

"Except…"

"Yeah?"

"I tried to talk to her. You know? About my feelings? It's really weird. She kept asking me to open up to her and talk to her, so I finally did."

"And?"

"Well, she hasn't said anything about it since then. She didn't comment at all. It's like she wasn't expecting me to say what I said. Or maybe she thought I'd say something else. I don't know." He looked perplexed.

"I never talk about my feelings," I said. "I try and be the strong silent type. John Wayne, you know? Except I cry over shit so easy they always see through me and know how deep I feel, so I really don't have to say anything. The good ones, the strong women, they appreciate it." I shrugged a good old fashioned American shrug and said, "Or maybe I'm just full of shit."

I walked him to the door again thanking him for retrieving my belongings. I didn't bother unpacking. I just went to bed and slept until I heard things going bump and bang and realized the guys were trying to wake me up with break-fall practice before breakfast. It worked.

After class I spent the morning catching up on business, doing laundry, and trying to organize. I'd been really disappointed to find that Curtis had not grabbed my Armani tuxedo, but knew that he would not have had a clue that it was mine. I hadn't told him about my trip to Monte Carlo. Losing that stung, I had to admit.

When the clock finally passed the 12:00 PM mark I got into my car and drove over to College Park on the near west side of Orlando. Opie Taylor had been doing late-night work and I'd decided to let him sleep. I parked on the street in front of his bungalow and walked up to the front door. It was quiet in the neighborhood and the only sounds were birds chirping and a dog barking far away. I waited for a moment and then whistled softly.

The front screen door exploded and a hundred pounds of tooth, fur, and pure unbridled love burst through and hurled itself at me. I dropped to my knees and grabbed his throat and wrestled him back and forth. He lunged up and nipped my ear and then threw himself onto me and then danced around me and finally whimpered as he lay in my lap.

"Nico, Nico, Nico…" I whispered over and over again. I looked up as I heard a high pitched barking above me and then Grindle, my little dachshund, was trying to reach me. I picked him up and held him close as he licked my face.

"If you ever find a woman who's that happy to see you, you should marry her."

"Fat chance," I said.

I stood and reached up and shook Opie's hand. Ellen Hunt, his lady friend kissed me on the cheek and we sat down on his wicker porch furniture.

"Thank you for keeping my dogs," I said.

"You're just lucky to get them back," Ellen said. "I just adore these two guys."

Nico had come up the steps and sat in front of me with his head resting in my lap. I scratched his ear and softly stoked his golden fur.

"Oh, I have something for you." I stood and went to the car. I brought back a tall box with a glass front and handed it to Opie. "Thank you."

"I told you we wouldn't take anything for watching these guys," he said. "It really is a pleasure to have them around."

"It isn't for that. It's for what you did for me in France."

"What is this?" Ellen asked, taking the box from Opie.

Opie said, "That, Sweetheart is the finest rum in the world. It's Gosling's family reserve. Hard to get and very expensive, it is like no other you will ever taste. Thanks, Parker, but what did I do in France?"

I looked at him and then glanced at Ellen. She stood and walked into the front room of the house saying, "I guess I'll let you two talk…" The screen door closed softly.

"Nice," I said. "In Garibaldi Square… Tuesday night?"

Opie shook his head. "I've never been there."

"You haven't?"

"Nope. I've never been to Nice. I've never been anywhere in France but Paris."

"Are you being coy?"

"No. What happened?"

I spent an hour telling him the whole story in all its sordid detail. Finally he nodded his head and smiled slightly.

"Well, I got a couple of very obscure test messages last week and I think this partly explains them. After we talked and I told you about the Musashi painting I called a guy I know. He was a guy I met in Fallujah during the war. He was on special assignment, you know, one of those mercenaries that show up for all the excitement and money that always seems to follow a war?"

"Yeah, I know."

"He's a good guy and a hell of a shooter. Actually he's pretty scary, but we got along and actually used to drink together sometimes. He made a name for himself in the French Foreign Legion."

"I didn't know they still existed."

"Oh, yeah, Parker. They do. Think Navy SEALs with an attitude."

"Yikes."

"Anyway, he told me he couldn't do anything because he was on lock-down in Damascus. There's a civil war there or something."

"Or something," I said dryly.

"He was tied up and just couldn't get away, so he put out a message on his, um… his cell? His network? Anyway he passed the word that he needed somebody to cover your back for a few days."

"Nice of him."

"Well, he kind of owes me."

"I don't even want to know."

"So then last Monday I got a message, a text that said… Well, here." He picked up his telephone and thumbed it for a few moments and then handed it to me. It read,

Parker's back is against the Wall and that was all.

I stared at it. "What's that supposed to mean?"

"I assumed it meant you were in trouble, so I tried to call Felix again, but I couldn't get through to him. I was worried, to tell you the truth. But then on Wednesday I got another message." He took the phone and thumbed it again and handed it back.

Tell him we're even

I stared at it for a moment and then began to smile.

"What?"

I looked at him and thought about telling him. Why not?

"I think I know who it is. Who it was with that gun…"

"Yeah? Who?"

"Opie, have you ever heard of a man named Thomas Wall?"

He frowned. "Who hasn't? Besides Carlos the Jackal he's probably the most famous, the most elusive and dangerous assassin in the world. I think he's…" He stopped and looked up sharply at me. "Against the Wall?"

I nodded.

"You know him?

I nodded again. Hair was rising on the back of my neck and I felt waves of both fear and appreciation wash through me.

"Thomas Wall? I can't believe it. How do you know him?"

"I did a little work for him up in Chicago. I got him out of a jam once, and he saved my ass once up in Montreal, although to be honest I wouldn't have needed my ass being saved if he hadn't been there."

"Thomas Wall?"

"Yeah, Opie. It makes sense. Who else could have followed me all over Nice and not been spotted? Who else could have fired a .44 from a hundred feet away and made that shot in the dark and the rain?"

"Parker, man, I'm getting goose bumps."

I thought about it. "I mean, there's the texts." I pointed at his phone. "Did you try to text him back?"

"Yeah, but the lines were disconnected."

"He has some kind of a system that opens telephone lines and you use them once and as soon as you hang up the line doesn't have any record of ever existing."

"That's convenient."

"It is if you don't ever want anyone to find you."

We were both quiet then.

"I'm glad you're safe and that he was able to take that shot."

I stood up and turned to walk to my car. "Me, too," I said.

Chapter 36

Five days before Christmas I looked up from reading a book to see a Fed Ex truck pull into my driveway. The place was otherwise quiet. The dojo was recessed for the holidays and wouldn't resume class until after New Year's Day. I watched the driver wearily climb out and bring a large package up the driveway. I walked down the porch steps and signed for it and told him to have a Merry Christmas. He nodded and trudged off.

I carried it into the house and tore off the paper covering it. A letter was taped to the box and I opened it. It was from Kara. She told me that after a lot of deliberation the French and Japanese authorities had agreed to a story and that she was allowed (with guards) to take the Musashi to Japan and present it to the head of her school at Hombu Dojo.

It was great press, after all, and the way it went down made everyone happy. There was a formal gathering and a big ceremony and then Doshu was supposed to take it to the Royal Palace or somewhere, and present it to a big shot representative of the Emperor and it was supposed to then belong to all Japanese people. She got her strokes and Doshu got a few and everybody was happy.

The Japanese government made a generous present to her for her troubles and when the annual Kagami Biraki promotions were announced it was disclosed that Doshu had raised Kara up to a level where, as she described it, she was, in American vernacular, running with the big dogs.

I was jealous. All Doshu had done for me was keep me out of jail for the rest of my life.

She went on to say that she wanted to give me something to show her appreciation for saving the Musashi and making everything possible for her. Her life was going to be much changed due to the money and promotion.

I opened the box and laughed.

She had sent me my own midnight blue Armani tuxedo. Typical Kara. Still, I was very glad to get it back and I knew I would be wearing it over the holidays. Fat Albert was always swamped by celebrities and in need of bodyguards to attend the Christmas parties and events. I'd be the best dressed guy in the room.

I laughed again and took it into the bedroom and dug around for a garment bag to keep it nice. After I'd hung it on hangers I was smoothing the jacket and felt a lump in the inside pocket. I dug into it and came out with what looked like a piece of bone. After I walked out to the porch to look at it in daylight I found it was not bone, but ivory.

It was finely carved with a chrysanthemum on each end and although it was delicate, it was also strong. It was also very old. I knew I was holding something that had been worn by the great Shogun Ieyasu Tokugawa. I took it to the mantle and set it there. I would find a suitable display case for it later.

And now I knew who had bought the set of netsukes and where they were. Well, that was on her, now, and I did not intend to ever get involved again. I was happy to have one and knew I would someday return it to Japan as well, but for now it made me happy to have it. It was a link to a past that was a different time and one that somehow I was bound up with and yet separate from.

I opened a beer and went back to the porch. My life was simple again. It was quiet. Nico came out and jumped up on the couch and then Grindle barked to be lifted up and join us.

In the driveway a silver car pulled in and stopped under the giant white bird of paradise. The trunk lid popped up and then the driver's door opened and I watched a gorgeous long leg slip out and then watched a tall blond woman go to the trunk. She picked up a suitcase and a bag of groceries and slowly walked up the driveway. She stopped when she got to the bottom step.

"I thought I'd come by and spend a few days. You aren't married are you? Got any other women coming by?"

I grinned. "No and no."

"Good." She climbed the stairs and set the suitcase by the open door and put the groceries on the steamer trunk in front of the windows. Then she was in my arms and I couldn't stop holding her. Finally she looked up at me and said, "Everyone went home. There we were in L.A. and we decided to take a long break for Christmas and everyone left and I realized I didn't have any place I wanted to be except here with you."

"It's okay, Baby. It's okay. Welcome home."

"Oh, Parker," she said. She kissed me and we stood like that for a long time.

Finally I picked up her suitcase and took it to the bedroom. She went into the kitchen to put away the groceries. I walked out of the bedroom and stood in the doorway and watched her.

"Hey, Monique," I said. "Let's go get a Christmas tree. I haven't had a Christmas tree here for years and it would make the old place feel really nice."

She smiled a huge, radiant, beautiful smile and said, "I thought you'd never ask."

Bogart. She was doing Bogart.

Special thanks to Steve Fasen and Francis Takahashi for their expertise in Japanese culture and willingness to share.

For anyone interested in paleoanthropology and ideas expressed in this novel I heartily recommend having a DNA analysis done by those great folks at the National Geographic Genome Project. So much information is coming so fast it is nearly impossible to keep up.

I read several dozen books preparing to write this novel. Most of the reading was a pleasure, to be honest. There are many books on paleontology that I could recommend, but anyone truly interested (in this day of Internet connectivity) can find as many titles and all the pertinent critiques that they could ever use. However there was one title that I found uniquely useful. *Before the Dawn* by Nicholas Wade is as deep, rich and clear as a glass of DRC and as enjoyable.

As Jimmy Buffett, that eminent sage and scholar one put it, *Anyone who does not spend at least a little time in France is cheating themselves out of one of life's great pleasures...* Unlike most of what comes out of his mouth, in this he is correct. The food, wine and simple pleasures of being there are something one should savor at least once.

And lastly, do look into an occasional geology textbook. The truth is out there.

Dan Linden,
Sangerville, Maine,
11/15/2013

33965435R00144

Made in the USA
Lexington, KY
17 July 2014